Faking
the
Dream

JJV: The Storyteller

Faking the Dream

Copyright © 2015 by JJV: The Storyteller
ISBN-13: 978-0-9978472-0-8 (Custom Universal)
ISBN-10: 0-9978472-0-4
LCCN: 2015942974

DEDICATION

This book is dedicated to my brother, Marcus, who I truly admire as a courageous black man and to all of us who continue to fight the fight, despite the naysayers, challenges, obstacles, and roadblocks thrown our way. The struggle is real, but keep up the fight.

ACKNOWLEDGEMENTS

I so wanted to skip this part for the third book, but realized that I have not been in this alone. I have received so much support along the way, and I need to express that I am appreciative to all of you that have contributed to me making this journey a successful one. Whether it was words of encouragement, prayers, spreading the word out about my novels, sharing your home with me, or physically picking up boxes to help me move, I love you and appreciate all that you have done. But in closing, I must recognize my Father, because I know that without Him, none of this would be possible.

INTRODUCTION

At twenty-five years old, most people would say that I am living the dream. The women, the cars, the homes, the parties, the money, the fame, but in reality, I don't really know how to dream anymore. I have hidden who I am from most people for all of my life. However, I have met the person who I feel can change my life forever — Porchia Williams. Six years ago, I let her slip right through my fingers by not being honest about who I am and what I am. I really still don't know what I am, except that I am unhappy and still looking to live the dream. Too many people expect too many things from me. My folks expect me to take care of them; my teammates expect me to lead them; my fans expect me to get the championship ring; women expect for me to marry them, and my boy toys expect me to come out of the closet.

I have never thought of myself as gay, or for that matter, not gay. I think of myself as a man who enjoys having sex with men. In the gay community, I am known as a b-boy. Although I did not start off liking sex with men, over the years, I have had a few satisfying sexual relationships, never intimacy, just sex. I really enjoy the wham-bam-thank-you-sir with a regular male sex partner. As for the women, I find myself either staying away from them or sexing as many of them as

I could tolerate. I would do anything to protect my status as a heterosexual male.

In my position as a professional NBA player, I can't afford for anyone to find out about my ambiguity when it comes to my sexual preference. I remember when Jason Collins came out and how the sports world reacted to his announcement. I don't want my career to be about the gay guy who led the NBA in assists, steals, rebounds, and three-pointers. The odd thing is, I can't even come out and say I am gay. I would have to come out and say, "I enjoy men sexing me down."

I feel that I am caught in a world that is unfamiliar to individuals within our society. We are accustomed to classifying individuals as gay, bisexual, transgendered, or transsexual, which all have nice, neat labels. However, I can't identify with any of these labels, although society would want to classify me as being bi-sexual. I reject this label because, more than anything, I desire to have an intimate relationship with a woman. However, I feel that a relationship with a woman would not be sustainable because she does not have the one tool that is necessary to provide me the same pleasure that a man can.

That is, until I met Porchia. Porchia makes me feel complete as a man. I don't long for anything when I am with her ... not even sex with a man. I was only nineteen years old at the time, but the first time I met her, I knew that she was the one for me. I'm ready to turn in my "gay" card and settle down with Porchia forever. Today, although she has moved on with her life, I still yearn for Porchia. I want to take you back to how my story began.

Chapter 1

My life started in a little town called Beaumont, Texas. It's located about eighty-four miles outside of Houston, Texas, and sixty miles from Lake Charles, Louisiana, where most of my family originated. My mom's great-grandmother and great-grandfather left Lake Charles because they thought there would be better opportunities in Texas. As the family journeyed to Houston, they stopped in Beaumont to visit family and decided that they would settle their roots there.

My mom's grandmother married a man who had inherited a lucrative cattle ranch business from his father that also doubled as a moonshine establishment. After a few years of running the business, he ended up losing everything, including his wife and kids, because of his gambling habit. My great-grandmother remarried a minister, and from this union, my grandfather was born. He was also a minister, and he married a minister's daughter. From that union, my mother, Anita Fontenot, was born. She was the youngest of six children and was considered the most rebellious from this union.

My mom had a very close relationship with her dad, but he died on her twelfth birthday. She and her mother had a very strained relationship after his death. My mom said that her mother told her repeatedly, if she could not follow the rules of the house, she would have to go, so that was exactly what she did. She met this older man named Tyrelle Gamble, who was an off-shoreman and moved in with him. He was gone most of the time, but paid all of the bills at the house. By fifteen, my mother was pregnant with me.

When her off-shoreman found out that she was pregnant, he ran out on the both of us. She later found out that he had a wife and two children that lived in the neighboring town of Port Arthur, Texas. Despite all of this, she named me Tyrese Gamble, after my absentee father. I often thought about finding him, but then I'd think, *For what? He knew where to find me if he was ever interested.*

My mother was a very proud woman and did not want to run back to her family or accept any form of welfare, so she decided that she would raise me by taking on odd jobs, such as housekeeping and babysitting for white folks. We did not have much money after she paid the rent. I remember that the best days were Mondays through Fridays because I was guaranteed a hot breakfast and a hot lunch at school. On the weekends, we got by on Malt-o-Meal, rice, Spam, bologna, government cheese, Kool-Aid, bread, and milk. My mom had to make her WIC vouchers last throughout the month.

My mom couldn't afford to buy me new clothes, so I wore a lot of hand-me-downs. I dressed so bad in the first and second grades that my first cousins would act as if they did not know me at school, although we spent most weekends playing together. On Sundays, I would wear my special hand-me-downs that came from the white folks my mom worked for. Most of the time, my shoes were worn and too tight. While other kids wore Nikes and Adidas, I sported no-name brands from Kmart. I remember one time getting some Chuck Taylors from the Goodwill store. I wore them until holes formed on the front and back.

I was bullied by other kids and was the butt of every "Yo-Momma-So-Po'" joke that I could have been more successful than Kevin Hart on those jokes alone. One of the ones I really remembered was, "Yo momma's so po' that you eat cereal with a fork to save the milk." Well, I remembered that one so well because I did eat cereal with a fork. Not to save the milk, but because we did not have any spoons. I rarely had the luxury of eating cereal, and my Malt-o-Meal was always so thick, it could only be eaten with a fork.

Despite having hand-me-downs and not enough food to eat, my mom tried to teach me values such as cleanliness, respect for others, the value of family, being thankful to God, and turning the other cheek. As I look back, I am not certain those were all good values because, after a lot of counseling, I now understand why I allowed some of the things to happen in my childhood that may not have otherwise happened, if I had not taken what my mom taught me to heart. My mom had nothing but good intentions, but as some have proclaimed, the road to hell is paved with good intentions.

Academically, I did well in school. Although my mother dropped out of school, she was a bright lady. She taught me how to read and write before I went to school. I also attended the Head Start program, so I was ahead of the other students when I entered kindergarten. My teachers wanted to skip me a grade ahead, but my mother told them that she wanted me to stay with my class because I lacked the social skills and maturity to deal with older students. By the time I entered third grade, I had the reputation of being both intelligent and diligent. I would ask my teacher to work with me on understanding class work, instead of going to recess. Recess was not my favorite activity anyway because I was just target practice for most of the other kids. I did not fight back because my mother told me "to turn the other cheek" and "that sticks and stones may break my bones, but words could never hurt me." When I got home, I would tell my mom about what happened at school, and she would just tell me that this was all part of growing up. I look back now and understand that I was bullied during my primary years. But I also understand what my mother was saying: "What does not kill you just makes you stronger."

By the time I entered fourth grade, life changed drastically for us. One of the families that my mother worked for had a son who was a doctor at Christus St. Elizabeth Hospital. They were fond of my mother and saw that, although she worked hard, she still struggled raising her young child. They convinced their son to help my mother get a job at the hospital as a janitor. That was where my mother met a nurse named Rico Valentin. Rico was a charismatic, suave, intelligent Puerto Rican who had moved from New York City to Beaumont to take a job as head nurse in the pediatric department at the hospital. My mother enjoyed telling the story about how Rico approached her at the hospital with a big smile, speaking Spanish because he thought she was Latina. She knew enough Spanish to say, "No hablo Español."

They quickly became friends; then shortly after that, they started dating. Once they started dating, Rico provided my mom with enough money, not only to put chicken on our dinner table, but for us to afford new clothes and shoes. We went from putting things on layaway at Goodwill to driving to JCPenney's to go shopping.

My mother, for the first time in her life, was able to purchase a used car. We had caught buses for so long that, when she first got the car, we walked to the bus stop to catch the bus to go grocery shopping. I looked at her and said, "Mama, why are we not driving?"

She just smiled, shook her head, took my hand, and we walked back to our apartment to get the car. After a few months of my mother dating Rico, we moved from our apartment in the projects to Rico's house in the Gladys Avenue/Dowlen Road area, where my mother used to clean houses for white folks.

The first month at Tio's (the name he'd told me to call him) was great. I had a roomful of toys, clothes, shoes, games, stereo, and a TV. It looked like Christmas every day at Tio's. Tio provided me and my mom with everything that we needed. I ate steak and shrimp for the first time in my life. My mom, for the first time in her life, smiled and laughed all the time. My mother had always been so busy trying to take care of me that she did not have time to enjoy life. Tio hired babysitters for me while he and my mother went out on date nights. This was the first time someone outside of my family watched me. However, even with all my new prized possessions and my new life, I missed my cousins, teachers, and, oddly, some of the bullies from my old school.

The fourth month at Tio's, my life drastically changed. I believe that everything that happens to a person contributes to the character that he or she develops and affects many of the decisions that one makes. In my case, this was when I began experiencing the nightmare that forever shaped my life and haunts me until this day. From this time on, I began avoiding the nightmare and faking the dream.

Chapter 2

It all started off so innocently, the nighttime reading of stories and tucking me in my bed. Then it went from tucking me in bed to touching my genitals after the reading. Then it went from touching my genitals to playing a game of "you touch me here, then I touch you there." I knew something was not right, but Tio convinced me that it was "what all boys did with their fathers." He made it seem like it was some type of rite of passage that led into becoming a man. He told me that I could never share this with anyone because men kept this between each other. According to Tio, it was an unspoken truth no one ever discussed.

Within a year, Tio was performing oral copulation on me and forcing me to do it back in return. This later led to him penetrating me from behind. It hurt so much the first few times that I could not sit or walk. When my mom asked me what was wrong, I told her that I could not use the bathroom. She gave me her home-based laxative of mineral oil that had me running to the bathroom for four days. At least, I had a short break from Tio putting his penis in my butt. The next week, he brought something in a tube, which I later learned was lubricant, and put it in my butt. That made the penetration much easier.

When I was about ten years old, my mother walked in right before he was about to do his act, but he was able to quickly explain to her that he had explained the birds and bees to me and was about to show me the male reproductive organs and how they worked. This should have set an alarm off for my mother, but she simply told him that she did not think that a "show-and-tell" was the best way to teach me about the male reproductive system. After almost being caught, Tio ceased doing what I later learned was termed rape. When I was twelve years old, he tried again, but this time, I fought back. It did not help because he overpowered me and raped me once again.

By this time, I knew that what Tio was doing to me was wrong. He threatened me with all sorts of horrific consequences if I told anyone, including killing me and my mom. It was difficult for me to tell at that point because I didn't know if anyone would believe me. Tio was a well-respected, charismatic man who was liked by all. Our family thought he was an angel who had rescued me and my mom from poverty. In fact, he was a devil in disguise who raped, abused, and tortured me for four years. When Tio bought me a basketball, I started spending as much time as I could on the court to get away from the abuse. I would go to school and not come home until I knew my mother was also home. There were times he caught me and still forced me to perform oral copulation, even when my mother was in the house.

I caught my big break when Rico was caught stealing drugs from the hospital and selling it on the streets. Even after his arrest, people still wanted to come to his aid. I was so glad when he was convicted and sent to prison for twenty-five years. It later came out that Rico had also abused some of the young boys on his floor when he was on duty. It was also discovered that he'd left NYC to come to Beaumont because the last hospital that he worked threatened to fire him and expose that he had sexually abused young boys. When all of this came out, I think my mother knew that I had also been sexually abused. But neither one of us ever spoke about it or mentioned Rico Valentin for a long time.

After Rico was incarcerated, I tried to forget about the abuse by eating, drinking, and sleeping basketball. By the time I entered junior high school, I was almost six feet tall and was pretty good at the sport. When I was not in school, I spent most of my time on the court. I also played on my junior high school's basketball team. It was odd to me that the same girls who made fun of me were now all trying to holler at me. They acted as if I was the best thing since grape Kool-Aid. I dodged them all based on how they used to treat me. I made a few friends at my new school, but still primarily hung out with my cousins.

I lived with my secret all through junior high school. I attempted to fit in and be a regular child. The fact was

I felt like an outsider, and often wondered whether other boys had experienced what I had experienced. I remember the first few times my basketball coach put his hand on my shoulder, I flinched, thinking that he was trying to make sexual advances toward me. It took me a while to get comfortable with an adult male touching me. When my coach would want to speak with me away from the team, I kept waiting for him to do what Rico used to do to me. I still questioned whether adult males did this toward younger males as a rite of passage, as Rico had told me. I wanted to talk to someone about it, but the only person I trusted was my cousin Poo Man. I did not quite know how to bring up the subject, since all he talked about was waxing girls' azzes. I wondered, *Was that what Rico had done to me — waxed my azz?*

I was really close to my cousin Poo Man, who was also an only child. He was eighteen months older than me. At the end of Poo Man's eighth grade year, he and his mother, my mother's only sister, moved to Houston. Any time I was out of school for vacation or holidays, I would spend time with Poo Man. In Houston, I had the opportunity to play with guys who knew how to hoop. Some of them played at the college level. I felt that I was more challenged on the court there than I was in Beaumont.

Poo Man would try to introduce me to girls, but I had no interest. He would say, "Man, those girls are crazy about you, while I can't even buy their attention."

I would always tell him that I had dreams that went beyond entertaining girls. The older I got, the more I wanted to tell Poo Man about what happened to me, but I was ashamed about my naiveté. I feared that people would think something was wrong with me.

By the time I graduated from junior high school, I had grown several inches and was already being scouted by several colleges. I spent most of my last year of junior high school dodging girls from junior high and high school. All the boys talked about what they were doing to girls, and I decided that I would try it.

There was one girl, Kayla, that all the boys wanted, but no one could seem to get her. I decided I would see if I could get Kayla to have sex with me. I understood that sex with a girl involved a boy putting his penis into a girl's vagina. The guys would talk about how they'd first kiss them, then put their fingers down their pants. This was the way that they usually got the girls to have sex with them.

Well, I asked Kayla to go with me to the park, and she agreed. I found an area where there were no other people. We talked for a little while; then I did what the other guys said they had done. I kissed her a few times. She stuck her tongue in my mouth. I was not quite sure what to do with it, so I nibbled it for a while. She looked at me and said, "You don't know how to kiss, do you?"

I played it off and said, "I don't like to kiss like that."

Then she said, "Let me show you how to do it right."

She put her lips up to mine, parted my lips with her tongue, and then began to rub her tongue against mine. She then took my tongue and began to gently suck it. As we were kissing, I remembered that the guys had told me that they would put their fingers down the girls' panties. I remembered that Rico would put his finger in my butt. So I put my finger down her pants and tried to put my finger in her butt.

She jumped up and screamed, "What the hell are you doing?"

I was dumb-founded. I did not know what I had done wrong. So I told her, "I'm sorry. I don't think you're ready for me."

I left her standing there and ran home. She later called and apologized and told me that she'd heard about girls doing anal, but she did not like that, but she would be willing to try it with me next time.

I told her that there would not be a next time because I was seeing a girl in Houston. I told her I felt guilty, and that was the reason I ran away. I was surprised at her response. She told me that she was down with that. I could keep my girlfriend in Houston, and she would be my Beaumont girlfriend. I think that this was the first time I realized that men could do as they pleased, and there would be a woman around to unconditionally accept what he said or did without any consequences.

Chapter 3

The summer before starting high school, I realized that I wanted to do something to set me apart from everyone else that played ball in my area, so I started growing locks. By the time I entered high school, I don't know if it was the locks, but I had girls and women just throwing themselves at me.

My cousins told me I had dollar signs written all over my forehead because of my basketball skills. I was making up so many stories about my girlfriend in Houston that I almost convinced myself that I had a girlfriend in Houston. But making up this story was the only way I thought I could keep my shame a secret. Until I met Clayton Alexander Burns during my sophomore year, I thought I would live with my shame alone forever. CB, as he was called at our school, was one of the most popular guys at Dunbar. He was the starting quarterback and captain of the football team. He dated the most popular girl at school, Brittany, who was the lead cheerleader of the cheerleading squad. Clayton was destined for fame and glory through an illustrious football career. He'd had teams scouting him since the eighth grade. It did not hurt that he was biracial and favored former NFL tight end Tony

Gonzalez. One night at a party, we began talking and found that we had a lot in common. He was also an only child being raised by a single mom.

However, unlike me, Clayton came from a family that had a lot of money. His mom was a trust-fund baby who decided that she would rebel against her family by having a relationship with a black man, which resulted in an illegitimate child — Clayton Burns. Clayton was the only male child born in a long line of females. Clayton's great-great-grandfather had found oil, and the family had been living off the royalties and lucrative investments for four generations. Clayton's grandfather's will allowed for the females to be given trust funds, but the first male born to one of his daughters was entitled to the bulk of his fortune, as long as he kept the last name Burns.

Over the next year, Clayton and I became really close and shared a lot, including the fact that we both were molested as children. Clayton was molested by his aunt's husband who served as his role model. Since Clayton did not have a father and his uncle did not have a son, they did a lot of things together, including attending sporting events. He traveled alone with his uncle on camping and fishing trips, hunting, skiing, and all sorts of other activities. Clayton said the abuse began when he was six years old. The first time it happened was when his uncle took him on a weekend camping trip. He sodomized him.

Every trip, thereafter, involved some type of sexual activity. Like me, Clayton did not know who to tell because he felt that no one would believe him. This abuse lasted until he was old enough to start hanging out with friends and telling his mother he did not want to go on trips with his uncle anymore. Clayton told me that I was the first person he had told about the abuse. Clayton's uncle died last year. Clayton said, on the day his uncle died, he felt that he could breathe again.

The day of his uncle's funeral, he hung back at the gravesite. His family knew that his uncle had treated him like his son, so they thought it would be appropriate for Clayton to have a few parting words with him. Clayton told me that he spat on his uncle's grave and cursed at him for about fifteen minutes. After leaving his grave site, he promised himself that he would not think about it again. But this turned out to be a lie.

Something about knowing that I was not the only one who had suffered this type of abuse by an older man made me feel closer to Clayton. We had a sort of unspoken love and trust in one another that I never developed with anyone else in high school. One night we attended a party, and we both had a little too much to drink. Instead of going home to my mother's house drunk, Clayton drove me to his house. Clayton's mom was gone for the weekend, and that was where it all began.

I am not certain who made the first move, but we engaged in full-blown sex for the entire night. Him doing me, me doing him, and us doing each other. I know that I was drunk, but it felt good. The next day, when I woke up, I was not certain where I was at. Then it all came back to me. I was immediately guilt-stricken.

He came into the room wearing nothing but briefs and eating a bowl of cereal. I quickly dressed and told him that I would see him later. I spent the whole next week avoiding him at school. I even started talking to more girls, pretending that I was interested in them. I did not know what was happening, but I knew that I did not like the idea of having sex with a guy.

The following week, I was at a burger joint with one of the females that I was pretending to like. She was all over me when Clayton and his girlfriend walked in. My date looked and saw it was Clayton and said to me, "Look who is here. I am going to call them over."

Before I could stop her, she yelled, "Hey, CB! Come on over and sit with us!"

Clayton came over, looked directly at me, and said, "Well, I don't want to interrupt your date."

I quickly responded, "It is not a date; we are just eating." I immediately regretted those words coming out of my mouth.

Brittany looked at him and said, "Come on, baby. It will be fun to have company."

The girls chatted while we sat. Every now and then, I looked up to find Clayton looking at me. I would quickly look away.

When the girls decided that they wanted to go to the bathroom, Clayton broke the awkward silence by saying, "Man. You did that the other day. Was that your all-time game high?"

I looked at him and said, "Yeah, I had a pretty good game."

He then looked at me seriously and said, "Look, man. We need to talk."

I responded, "About what? We cool."

"No, we not. You been avoiding me ever since that happened."

"Nah, man. We cool," I said.

Just as he was about to say something else, the girls returned to the table, giggling. My date said, "Why don't we go bowling?"

"Well, I got some homework to do," I quickly said

"But it is the weekend. We don't have school tomorrow," my date responded.

I looked at her and said, "Yeah, but I have a weekend tournament. I won't be able to do my homework."

"I will do your homework for you. I want us to have a little fun tonight."

Brittany grabbed my hand and said, "Puleeze! You know you can get away with not doing any homework. All the teachers love you."

Brittany was right, but I did homework because I wanted to stay on top, both in my school subjects and basketball. After all of the pleading, I gave in to the peer pressure.

I actually enjoyed our double date. Clayton and I acted like we did during old times, high-fiving and making fun of each other. A couple of the other students we knew came over and joined us. Before I knew it, we had a party going on at the bowling alley. I had my mother's car, so I told them that I had to cut out because my mom expected me back by ten o'clock. My date was really enjoying herself, so I asked Clayton if he minded taking her home. He agreed, and when I told her that Clayton would take her home, she seemed happy and said that she appreciated me considering her feelings. I took note that my date would definitely be worth hanging out with again … if only I could have remembered her name.

Clayton called me a few days later and asked if I could meet him at his house. I told him I could meet him, but that I would like to meet him at a neutral spot. We agreed to meet at a soul food/jazz venue in downtown Beaumont. I thought we were known in our neighborhood and schools, but it was funny that a couple of the patrons recognized both me and Clayton and engaged in discussions about football and basketball while we were at the downtown spot. Clayton and I talked about some of the things that were happening at school and who was offering him scholarships. This went on for several minutes before he finally got to the point of why he wanted to talk.

"Hey, man. I want to apologize for my actions."

"Man, forget it. We both had too much to drink."

"I may have had too much to drink, but I knew what I was doing."

"What do you mean?" I asked.

"Look, you're not the first guy I have had sex with."

"Yeah, I know you were abused," I said.

18

"No, I had consensual sex with other guys after that."

"What?" I asked.

"Yeah, I need to keep up my heterosexual image for football."

"Man, you got me twisted. I ain't no fag."

"I take offense to that word. I ain't a fag either."

"But what about Brittany?"

"I just have to use her to fit the image."

"Man, I ain't down with this homo shit."

"Well, we are friends, and I thought I should let you know what's up with me."

"Does anyone else know at school?" I asked.

Clayton responded, "No. And I hope that you will keep it that way."

"Yeah, man. You can trust me. I am just not interested."

"I am interested in you, but I understand. Hope we can still be friends."

"Bet."

We banged fists, ordered dessert, and went back to talking about sports.

Chapter 4

One night, I was hanging with Clayton and some other guys from the basketball and football teams. We all had had a lot to drink, and Clayton and I ended up in his bed again. He looked at me and asked whether it was going to be consensual this time. I told him that I wanted it as much as he did. That night, Clayton and I began our sexual relationship.

Our relationship was purely physical. Not once did we kiss or touch each other outside of stimulating ourselves for intercourse. During our relationship, I enjoyed receiving more than giving. Clayton enjoyed both, so I had to make certain I geared myself up for stroking him as good as he stroked me. With the exception of the first time I fell asleep in his bed, we always parted once we were physically satisfied.

In the meantime, I dated girl after girl until I was labeled Player of the Year for more than basketball. I would go on a couple of dates then move on to the next one. Not once did I have sex with any of them. If they had talked to each other, they would have known. I guess each of them felt that they just did not meet up to the standards of Tyrese Gamble, and I suppose, none of them wanted to expose themselves to what they felt were their shortcomings.

Not once did I meet any girl in high school that could keep my interest. I felt bad because they paid for most of the dates and bought me things that I never wanted. I found that the white girls were even more willing to please me than the sistas. I said to myself at that time, if I had to fake an ongoing relationship with anyone, it would be with a white girl.

I met up with Clayton, at least, once a week to get my fix. Graduation time for Clayton came all too fast for me. He wanted me to attend Senior Day and the prom with him, so I had to find a senior that would ask me out to Senior Day and the prom. We together decided that the best person for me to pursue would be Vernita Haygood.

Vernita was a very beautiful, shy, smart girl whose father was a minister. We figured that I would not have to deal with the pressure of her pushing me into having sex with her. It was odd for me at first, because I had never really pursued any girl before; they were always running after me. It was difficult to convince Vernita that I was genuinely interested in her because she was not part of the "in-crowd." It took me about a month before she agreed to go out with me.

Vernita told me that I would have to meet her parents before they would allow her to go out with me. Reverend Haygood was known to rip guys apart. When I first met him, I was shaking and could barely speak. He looked at me and said, "Boy, get your senses about you! I am not going to beat you down!" Then he smiled, grabbed my shoulder and said, "At least, not yet. And I won't as long as you do my daughter right."

I wanted to just bolt right then and there, knowing that I did not have good intentions toward his daughter. As a matter of fact, I had no intentions toward her at all. Instead, I looked him directly in his eyes and said, "Sir, I have nothing but respect for you and even more respect for your daughter."

From that moment on, Reverend Haygood greeted me with a hug. And I learned how to fake sincerity.

My first date with Vernita went well. She was intelligent, so I could speak to her about a number of subjects, with the exception of sports. She knew that I played basketball but did not understand anything about the game. She knew that the object of the game was to put the ball through the hoop, so I spent a lot of our dates explaining the game and the job of each position. After explaining to her the key positions on the team, I was impressed with her questions. She asked questions about the game such as, why is there a need for a center if you have a strong power forward? After a few dates, I really started liking Vernita as a person, but nothing else.

Vernita asked me to attend Senior Day and prom with her, just as Clayton and I had planned. Senior Day was a day at a water park in Houston. Vernita, who had gone unnoticed all during high school, became the envy of a lot of girls. Although she was beautiful, no one noticed because she wore glasses, homely clothing, and didn't talk much. Within the few weeks that we had been "dating," Vernita started wearing contacts, letting her hair down, and dressing a little less homely.

When Vernita took off her clothes at the water park, every girl and boy just stared. She had a body that most girls would kill for and that most guys would want to explore. She had my mouth wide open at how fine she looked in her bikini. The guys were talking shit to me all day about how they envied me for hitting that. Clayton revered at the attention that I received and smirked at me the entire trip.

By the time prom arrived, Vernita and I were giving Clayton and Brittany a run for their money. Brittany was not crazy about Vernita because Vernita was getting more attention at school than she was. It also did not help that Vernita stole the show at the prom with her dress. I was not certain how Reverend Haygood let her out the house like that because she left nothing to the imagination. I wanted to take off my jacket to cover her up. To top everything off, Clayton and Vernita won homecoming king and queen.

Vernita, Clayton, and I had a good time at the prom while Brittany sat pouting. Clayton rented a limousine and a suite at a hotel in Houston for an after-party. Brittany faked being sick and asked that we take her home. I guess Brittany thought the party would end, but Vernita slurred, "Let's get this party started. 'Cause one monkey won't stop my show."

So Vernita, Clayton and I rolled to Houston in the limo to some luxury hotel in downtown. We drank and smoked weed the entire way. By the time we arrived, we could hardly walk.

The suite had a ten-jet Jacuzzi tub big enough for six people. The first thing we did was take off all of our clothes and jumped into the Jacuzzi. Vernita started kissing me, while Clayton started kissing her on the back of her neck. Next thing I knew, Vernita was sucking my dick, while Clayton was hitting her from the back. I wondered whether he was in her butt or her pussy. I asked no questions because she was working my dick over well. She stopped sucking my dick and went to sucking Clayton's dick, while Clayton took his finger and started fingering me in my butt. I was concerned about Vernita seeing, but she was so into what she was doing that she would not have noticed if the roof caved in.

We left the Jacuzzi and made it over to the bed. The entire sex scene continued with Vernita being in the middle of me and Clayton. But not once did I penetrate Vernita or even have any interest to do so. I wanted Clayton to penetrate me so bad, I could have hollered. Instead I had Vernita suck my dick, while putting her fingers in my butt. That seemed to turn her on as much as it did me. We fell asleep intertwined, with Vernita wrapped up in the middle.

When we woke up the next morning, I thought that Vernita would be embarrassed by what she had done. Instead, she woke up, saying, "Hey guys, let's take a shower with me in the middle."

It was then I realized that Vernita was an undercover freak. We did not want to disappoint her, so we complied with her wishes.

On the ride back from Houston to Beaumont, Vernita was very chatty. I was hung over and did not have a lot to say. But Clayton indulged her, and they talked about a variety of subjects. When we arrived back in Beaumont, we took Vernita home first. She looked at us before getting out and said, "Guys, what happened between us will stay between us, right?"

We both looked at her and nodded our heads. When she closed the door, Clayton and I fell out laughing. Clayton looked at me and said, "Dayuum, Ms. Vernita Haygood earned her title. She does it 'in the hay good'!"

When we returned to school on Monday, Vernita came up to me and hugged and kissed me like she had been doing for the past few months. I kissed her back and told her that I needed to talk to her after school. I asked Vernita to meet me at Lovers' Lane. She tried to get me to tell her what I wanted, but I told her that it could wait. The real deal was that I was tired of faking it, so I did not need Vernita anymore.

Lover's Lane was a private spot that many of the students went to make out near the football field. When we got there, she started to kiss me, but I held her back. She looked at me with a frown on her face and said, "What's up, baby?

I looked at her in her eyes and said, "You are a great person, but you are not the type of girl I am looking for."

"Are you breaking up with me because I had a threesome with you and Clayton?" she screamed.

I responded, "Yes."

She shouted loudly, "You bastard!"

She then balled up her fist and punched me straight in the mouth, splitting my lip to the point that blood started gushing out. I wiped the blood with my shirt.

She then looked at me and said, "You better be glad I don't have a gun 'cause you would not be able to wipe the blood away."

She started crying and shaking. I went to hug her, but she jerked back and said, "Son of a bitch, if you touch me, I will be the last person that you eva touch again!"

She proceeded to fix her clothing, wiped her eyes, and walked away. That was the end of my charade with Vernita Haygood.

Chapter 5

My senior year was difficult, in part, because Clayton left to go to Washington State to play ball, but mostly because I was ready to enter the next phase of my life. I signed a Letter of Intent to play basketball with Miramar State and could not wait to begin college. Not for basketball, but to get closer to my goal of becoming a child psychiatrist. I have a good heart, but I came to realize that I was a fucked up person, and I was fucking with other people's lives. Children that are abused need assistance to be able to live healthy, productive lives.

My family became much closer to me and my mom once they figured I was headed toward a NBA career. My absent uncles, all of a sudden, wanted to play an instrumental role in my life by giving me advice. I had many more cousins than I'd ever imagined. Most of the family, including extended family, attended all of my games during my senior year. We had a whole section of Fontenots at every home game, and some who followed us on the road. In hindsight, I am certain I was not related to a lot of them, but it was cool to have the support.

However, my mom was always my biggest supporter. No matter what happened, I knew that I could depend on her. She still would go without buying the things she liked and enjoyed so that she could provide for me. I looked at her with nothing but love and admiration, although I did not necessarily agree with all of her values that she thought were based on biblical teachings.

I graduated with honors and was recognized for my contributions to the game of basketball by a number of organizations. But my mother was probably the proudest of me when I decided that I wanted to be baptized before I left for college. She had a celebration fit for a king on the day I was baptized. It was nice seeing all of our family come together at our home that my mom had purchased after we left Rico's.

We all seemed to be in a good place. But on this day, I could not help but reflect on my leaving Beaumont. I was sad about leaving my mother, but knew she had a renewed and strong relationship with her family, and they would be her support system in my absence. As far as I knew, my mom had not been involved with another man since Rico was incarcerated. I often wished that she would find someone that she could share her life with. She seemed content with God, me, and her family. I could not help but think that, after I left, loneliness might set in.

I was packing to leave for Virginia when my mother came and sat on my bed with a concerned look on her face.

I asked her, "Mom, what is wrong?"

She looked at me and said, "I am so sorry baby."

"Mom, what are you sorry about?" I asked.

"I should have known what that man was doing to you when I caught him with his pants down in your room."

I did not know how to respond. We had not spoken about Rico in years. I did not know why, on this day, she decided to tell me that she knew what happened. I was better off thinking that she had no idea.

"Mom that was a long time ago, and it was not your fault."

"Yes, it was my fault. A mom should know those types of things."

"Moms are not omniscient. You are human, although you have always been superhuman to me."

"Baby, you are always giving me a pass, but I am responsible. I should have gotten you counseling to get you through those rough times."

"Mom, I made it through. We barely had enough money to just make it through the day."

"Baby, you don't seem to have a normal relationship with any of your peers. I don't see you with any friends. And you have never had a girlfriend."

"Mom, I don't bring them here, but I do have friends. I just don't like people in my personal space. And I guess I am just like you. You don't have any friends."

"Boy, don't turn this around. I am old. You have a whole life ahead of you."

"Mom, I would not call thirty-four old. As a matter of fact, maybe we both need to go online to find someone."

"Boy, you know I will not go on a dating line. God will send me the right person."

"He will not if you don't go anywhere but to work and church."

"Well, I guess that's where my mate will come from."

"I don't know, Mom. Work messed you over last time," I said, smiling.

"Please don't remind me."

I hugged her and said, "You are a great mother, and you did an awesome job raising me. I love you now and forever."

"You are the greatest son anyone could ever have. I never deserved a son like you."

At that moment, I did not know how I could leave her alone. I started thinking that maybe I could rescind my Letter of Intent and go to junior college, so I could stay close to home. Then I remembered that I owed a lot, not just to myself, but to other children. I needed to be in a position to help abused children become productive members of society. In my sociology class, I'd read that eighty percent of children who are abused have some type of psychological disorder, some more severe than others. My goal was to decrease this percentage through my works.

Before leaving Beaumont, I thought about writing a letter to every female that I had hurt or used during my time in high school, asking them for their forgiveness. I wrestled with this thought in my head and decided that, instead, I would pray to God, and ask Him for His forgiveness. My hope was that His forgiveness would be extended to my many victims.

I also asked God to help me become a better person and to treat every individual I encountered with dignity and respect. I had done some heinous things to females in high school; things that, until this day, I am ashamed to discuss. I knew I wanted to leave Beaumont as a different person.

I was just about packed when my mom came in and said, "Tee, you have a visitor. I am about to leave for work."

I came out and kissed my mom, and she ran out the kitchen door, into the garage. I went to the living room, and there was Vernita and a baby. I must have looked at her like she was an alien.

She quickly said, "Hi, Ty. I heard that you were leaving for school in Virginia, so I wanted to come by and introduce you to your child before you left. We moved away to Houston, but I thought she should meet her daddy, at least, once."

"Vernita, that can't be."

"Yes, and here is your proof," she said, lifting the child.

"Vernita, you and I never had sex."

"Oh! Did you forget about prom night?"

"Vernita, we never had intercourse."

"Oh, I guess that this baby was an immaculate conception."

"No. If that baby's anybody's, it's CB's. You got the wrong person."

She looked visibly upset and said, "This is your baby. Look at her! She looks just like you!"

I looked at the baby, and she did look more like me than Clayton. But I told her that I was positive that we did not have sex that night. To calm her down, I told her I would be willing to take a DNA test to prove what I already knew.

She looked at me and said, "Don't you want to know her name?"

I really did not care what her name was because I knew she was not my baby. But I looked at the baby again and said, "She is a cutie. What is her name?"

"I named her Tyreesa Vernetta Haygood," Vernita said, smiling.

I was relieved to hear that she did not use Gamble as the surname for the bastard child.

I asked Vernita, "Why are you just now coming forth?"

"I moved to Houston to attend Texas Southern. Shortly after starting school, I realized that I was pregnant. I started dating a guy at TSU that I really liked. Instead of causing drama, I told him that the baby was his. But I know that I was pregnant before I left for Houston. And I am positive that you're my baby daddy."

I looked at her and said, "Well, we'll find out soon enough if she is mine. I was packing, so I need to get back at it. Thanks for coming by."

I then asked her for her phone number, gently nudged her toward the door, and told her I would be in contact soon.

Immediately after Vernita and her baby left, I called my cousin Poo Man. Poo Man was my go-to-man in times like this. He convinced me to go and take a DNA test as soon as possible. His words were: "Mane, you need to know if you have a little shorty running around before you sign that big contract. You may need to marry that ho. That's why I always told you, a ho can't do nothing for me but suck my dick."

I called Vernita and asked her if we could take the test tomorrow. She agreed, and I submitted my DNA right before I caught my plane to Virginia. I worried that perhaps I did not remember everything about that night. I knew my life would be forever changed if that baby was mine. I thought about calling Clayton and giving him a heads-up. But after Clayton left for Washington, I'd only heard from him twice. I figured if the baby was Clayton's, Vernita would find a way to get in touch with him when that time came. I swore, on that day, I would never have unprotected sex again, with neither a man nor a woman. Until then, I prayed that I was not the baby's daddy.

Chapter 6

I arrived in Virginia with a lot of enthusiasm. But I quickly figured out I was a long way from Texas. The school was located on the north side of Norfolk that had several other universities. The neighborhood was a little more diverse than what I experienced in Beaumont, or even Houston. Virginia reminded me more of the East Coast, than of the South. Once I arrived on campus, I was greeted by so many people, committees, and student organizations that it made my head spin. Although I had already met the coach and other staff, I was anxious to meet my teammates.

I was looking forward to the playing with some of the most highly rated basketball players in the NCAA. The Miramar State basketball team was comprised mostly of third and fourth year players. I was going to be the only freshman in the starting line-up. Miramar aggressively recruited me because their starting forward had graduated, and they didn't have anyone to fill that position. That made me nervous because these guys had been playing at the collegiate level for a while. They had made the Final Four three out of the last five years. They were also slated to win it all this year, and

I was expected to be a pivotal player in making certain that happened.

Because I was a freshman, I expected that the other guys would put me through some type of hazing or, at least, some type of test. Everyone was welcoming toward me and told me that they were looking forward to what I could bring to the team. It was important to me, not to let them down. It was the first time that my teammates and I developed close personal relationships. The entire starting lineup would hang out together all the time, in addition to the fifty hours a week we spent practicing on the court or working out in the gym. The team was really disciplined, and we worked hard, but also played hard.

When we found the opportunity to party, we would party from sundown to sunrise. I did not meet anyone that I was interested in sexually until I met Lisa Duvall. Lisa was a third year student on a journalism scholarship, who was originally from Harlem. She was very attractive and intelligent with an interesting street edge. She had a smooth chocolate complexion, long legs, a curvy body, and wore her hair in long natural ringlets.

My first exposure to Lisa was through an article that she wrote about me that was not very flattering. She said, "The highly sought-after player, Tyrese Gamble, proved that he possesses the skills to take Miramar to that next level long before His Majesty arrived. However, I think that his arrogance and self-absorbed nature may be an impediment to the game. His confidence in his own abilities and his lack of trust in his teammates demonstrated during his high school years will make it more difficult for Miramar to get the ring that they so honorably deserve."

I had been waiting to meet up with Ms. Duvall for some time. She was actually Gaylon's, the starting point guard for Miramar, girlfriend's cousin. I was talking to Gaylon and Erica when Lisa walked up and hugged Erica. She said hello to Gaylon, and Gaylon was about to introduce us when Lisa said, "Oh, an introduction is not necessary. Who would not know the notable Tyrese Gamble?"

I pretended that I did not know who she was when Erica said, "Ty, this is my gregarious cousin, the school newspaper's editor and writer, Lisa Duvall."

"Oh, this is the Lisa Duvall that wrote that very interesting article about His Majesty," I said.

Lisa looked and said, "Oh, so you do read?"

"Yeah, I learned how to do that last year."

Lisa laughed and said, "Ha! I see Tyrese Gamble also has a sense of humor."

"Yes, and my friends call me Ty."

Lisa hugged Erica and Gaylon and kissed them bye. Before walking away, she looked at me and said, "Well, it was nice to meet you, Tyrese."

I looked at Erica and said, "She is a tough one, I see."

"No, she is just pretending to be. She is very soft inside," said Erica.

That was the day I decided that I would have to get Lisa on Ty's team. Lisa was tough, but I had charmed enough girls in Beaumont to know how to get beyond that tough exterior. I eventually convinced Lisa to go out on a date with me. I found her to be much more interesting than many of the girls I had run across.

She was ambitious, knew sports, history, politics, music, art, world events, and nothing would stand in her way as she made it to the top. Within a month, Lisa and I were inseparable. Between the team, school, and Lisa, my life was not mine anymore. We were having a great relationship until Lisa tried to perform oral sex on me, and I rejected her.

"So what's wrong, Ty? You don't like me like that?"

"No, Lisa, I do like you like that!"

"Then why have you not made any advances toward me beyond a kiss?"

"I was not sure you were ready."

"You must not find me attractive."

"What man would not find you attractive?"

"Am I too aggressive for you?"

"You know that is what attracts me to you, besides those beautiful long, chocolate legs," I said while trying to nibble on her legs.

"I am tired of hugging, holding, kissing, and teasing."

"Well, I will give you whatever you want."

"No, I want you to want it too. Usually I have to fight off guys. Not beg them!"

"I'm sorry. I did not think you were ready."

She looked me directly in my eyes and squealed, "Oh, my God, you're a virgin!"

I did not deny or confirm her statement, but from that day forward, she stopped trying to get me to have sex with her. She was somewhat right. I was a virgin since I had never had sex with a girl.

Chapter 7

As busy as my schedule kept me, I made certain that I made time for my mother every day. I would call her, and she was always so happy to hear from me. I felt guilty for leaving her, knowing it was us against the world. But one day I called her, and she did not sound so good. The next day I called her, and got no answer. I tried her cell phone and still no answer. I got worried, so I called my grandmother, who informed me that my mother was in the hospital. I fussed at my grandmother for not calling me and letting me know. But she told me my mother had begged her not to call me. She said that my mother said that she did not want for anyone to bother me. She assured the family that she would be out of the hospital in no time.

I called Poo Man and he said that they had only found out a few hours ago, and he and his mom were leaving for Beaumont within the hour. I told Poo Man that I would find a way to get there. Poo Man convinced me to stay at school until he called to let me know what was going on. I trusted Poo Man, so I anxiously awaited his call. I was preoccupied during practice, so Coach pulled me aside and asked me what was going on. I explained to him what happened. He told me that family always comes first, so if I needed to get away to check on my mom, he understood.

Before I finished practice, Poo Man called. He left me a message on my phone, asking me to call him as soon as I got the opportunity. I was supposed to be meeting with my study group right after practice, but I decided that I would call Poo Man back before meeting with them. When Poo Man answered the call, I heard all types of commotion in the background. He told me he would have to call me right back. I waited for what felt like fifteen minutes before Poo Man called back.

The first thing he said when I answered the phone was, "Mane, you need to get here. It ain't good."

"What happened?"

"She has pneumonia, and the doctor said it doesn't look good."

I left and did not have time to contact anybody but Coach. He said that he would take care of everything. He asked me to call him when I arrived in Beaumont. Although Coach was a very rigid, discipline man, he acted as a father-figure toward his players.

When I arrived in Beaumont, I called him to let him know that I had arrived safely, and that I would be back in touch to let him know what was happening. I remembered that I had a date with Lisa, and I had not told her what happened. I called Lisa, and she sounded very concerned. She asked me whether she could join me, and I told her that was not necessary because I probably would be back soon.

When I arrived at the hospital, the Fontenots were there in full force. Even the little children were there running around in the family's waiting room. I was anxious to find my mother, so I attempted to avoid all of them. Poo Man previously texted my mother's room number to me, so I went directly to her room. When I arrived, the minister and my grandmother were in the room with my mom. I walked in, and my mother looked and said, "Baby, why are you not in school?" She was barely able to get the words out.

"I had to hunt you down because you did not answer my phone call!"

I went and kissed my grandmother and greeted the pastor.

"Baby, I'm sorry. I have no battery," my mother muttered.

She was having a difficult time talking. I could not believe she was talking about not having a battery when she was lying there with several IVs in her arms.

I walked over to kiss her and told her, "Mom, it's okay. I was worried, but I just want you to get better."

"I'm going to be just fine Love. Just need to get my strength back."

"With God's help, you will be better in no time. I'm going to have to go on and visit some other folks in here. But I will be checking back on you," said Pastor Riggins.

As the pastor was leaving, he told me he was proud of me and was looking forward to some great things from me. My grandmother decided to walk the pastor out. I was relieved because I wanted to speak with my mother alone.

"Mom, are you really okay?"

"Baby, I am doing much better…" She stopped and caught her breath. "…since I see you."

"Okay, don't talk anymore. I just want to sit with you," I said.

"Baby, I don't want you sitting here looking over me," she said as if she was taking her last breath. "I need for you to be in school."

I knew I wasn't going anywhere until I found out what was going on with my mother. I decided that I would go talk to the doctor. I said, "Mom, I will be back in a few minutes."

She just nodded her head as if she could not speak anymore. I went to the nurse's station to find out if the doctor was around. The nurse told me that the doctor was doing rounds and was expected back in about forty-five minutes. I explained to her that I was Anita Fontenot's son and I had just arrived from Norfolk, Virginia, and would like to talk with him about my mother's condition as soon as possible. She told me she would send him a text, so he could be aware that I was waiting to speak with him.

I took advantage of this time to go and greet the rest of my family. My uncle Pigeon was the first to notice me, and he ran over to greet me. Once I entered, the rest of the clan came and greeted me like I was a rock star. I kissed Aunt Verdie, spoke to my other uncles, joked around with my cousins, and played around with the kids for a minute, until I found the opportunity to dash out of the room, back to my mother's room. I stopped by the nurse's station before going into the room, and the nurse I'd spoken with previously told me the doctor would be ready to speak with me in five minutes near the cafeteria's entrance. She told me the doctor was an Asian man named Dr. Lee.

When I went back to my mother's room, she seemed to be peacefully sleeping, so I decided to walk down to the cafeteria to meet Dr. Lee. When I got there, Dr. Lee was already waiting. I walked up to him and asked him whether he was Dr. Lee. He greeted me with a smile and said he had heard a lot about me. I thought it was odd because I knew nothing about him.

He said, "Please follow me to my office."

While walking, he engaged in conversation about school and basketball. My body was there walking with him, but my mind was light years away, wondering what was wrong with my mother.

When we arrived at his office, I said, "Dr. Lee. I don't mean to be rude. But let's stop the small talk. What is wrong with my mother?"

"Well, your mother has AIDS, which has advanced to the last stage."

"What the hell are you talking about?" I asked.

"Your mom is at the stage where she can no longer fight off infections. We are doing everything to help fight the disease, but her immune system is not cooperating."

"How long has this been going on?"

"By the time your mom came to be diagnosed, she already had fully blown AIDS.

"Doctor, she never showed any symptoms. I don't remember her even being sick."

"Your mom probably had been suffering silently."

"So what can you do to make sure that she is okay?"

"I am sorry. The prognosis is not good, but we are going to do everything we can do to keep her comfortable."

"Damn, doctor! Are you telling me that she is dying! How did she get AIDS? Is it because she worked at this hospital?"

"We discussed that, and she told me she had no contact with anyone that had AIDS or that was HIV-positive. She also said that she has had only two sexual partners in her entire life."

The minute Dr. Lee said two sexual partners, I realized who it was. That motherfucker Rico had AIDS! I banged on the doctor's desk and said, "I will kill that muthafuka!"

Dr. Lee looked very surprised and said, "If you know who your mother may have contracted the virus from, we need to be able to get in contact with him."

I felt very vulnerable at that time and told the doctor the story about Rico. He told me that I immediately needed to be tested. He arranged for me to get tested that day. I sat with my hands in my face wondering, *How much more damage can one man cause?* I immediately went to the lab to get a blood test. The technician told me that the results should be available in thirty minutes. After the test, I went back to my mom's room and just hugged her with tears rolling down my eyes. She looked up and said, "Baby, it's in God's hand now."

I stayed with my mother until she fell asleep. Then, I went back to our house, which seemed cold and foreign to me. I walked in wishing that I had bought some Courvoisier before going home. I went to the kitchen and found an old bottle of red wine that someone had given my mother several Christmas' ago. I did not care if it tasted like vinegar; I just needed a drink.

I looked on the side of the refrigerator where my mom usually kept the mail. I grabbed the pile and started sorting through it. I saw a letter addressed to me from Abbott Labs. This is the lab that I had used for the DNA test for Vernita's baby. I'd had enough bad news for one day, so I did not want to open it. I decided that I would shower, then head for bed.

I woke up the next day thinking about everything that was going on. I determined it was better to know than not to know. First, I decided to go to the kitchen to open the DNA test results for Vernita's baby. My heart started beating really fast, and I had to talk myself into opening the envelope.

After about ten minutes, I opened the envelope and it read:

The alleged father is excluded as the biological father for the child named above. This conclusion is based on non-matching alleles at the loci listed above with a PI equal to zero. The alleged father lacks the genetic markers necessary to be the biological father of the child. The probability of paternity is 0.0%.

Under normal circumstances, this would have been the best news in the world. However, my mom was in a hospital bed dying, and I could be next. I'd spent time cussing at Rico, but knew that it was counter-productive. Knowing that my time with my mother may be short, I rushed to the hospital to spend time with her.

When I arrived at the hospital, nurses were running around like mad people. When I got closer, I could see they were running into my mother's room. I ran toward the door only to be held back by a big Samoan nursing assistant. He told me that I would only be in the way, and the best thing I could do was let the doctors and nurses attend to my mother. I asked him what was going on, and he told me that he did not know. I attempted to stop the next nurse that ran in, but she acted as if I was invisible. She completely ignored me as she ran into the room. I stood back, feeling helpless.

Dr. Lee came out twenty minutes later and said, "I am so sorry. We were unable to bring her back. She stopped breathing."

He went on saying something else, but I was not certain what he was saying. I pushed past him and went into the room. There she was, lying lifeless.

I screamed, "Mama! Mama!"

As two nurses attempted to grab me, Dr. Lee told them to give me time with her. I sat, holding her hand crying and telling her how much I loved her. It seemed like the staff came within minutes and rolled her body out of the room. I later found out that they gave me forty-five minutes to say good-bye.

Dr. Lee approached me as I was leaving my mother's room to tell me that I tested negative. I should have been celebrating two wins — no child and no HIV. However, at that time, it really did not matter. I had just lost the love of my life.

Chapter 8

Returning to school immediately after my mother's funeral was the best thing I could have done at that time. I was so tired of the overbearing family that thought they were on suicide watch and that they had to be around me twenty-four/seven. As far as the funeral, my grandmother took care of all of the arrangements. All I had to do was show up at the place and time that they told me.

Once I arrived back on campus, I put everything I had into school and basketball. I avoided Lisa because I knew she would want to pry into what happened, and I was not ready to discuss the circumstances surrounding my mother's death. She finally caught up with me as I was leaving practice one evening.

When I walked out, she had her hands on her hips, saying, "What does a sista have to do for a brotha to return her call?"

"Hey, Lees. I'm sorry. It has been crazy. I have just been trying to catch-up with practice and classes."

"Too busy to just say hi?"

"I'm sorry. What are you up to?" I asked.

"Just checking on you. What are you doing?" she said.

"About to meet with my study group."

She had such a defeated look on her face when she said, "Okay. Call me when you are free."

I grabbed her arm and said, "Forget that study group. Right now, I need to spend some time with my girl."

"Look. You don't have to do anything that you don't want to do. Obviously, you're not into me the way that I'm into you."

I was not feeling a fight with her, so I kissed her passionately. When I let her up for air, I asked, "So where is your roommate?"

"Oh, so you did miss a sista?" Lisa said, smiling and grabbing my hand.

Lisa lived in off-campus student housing that was within close proximity to the campus. We walked to her apartment and found that it was empty. Lisa asked if I wanted something to drink, and I told her yes. She brought me a glass of champagne. We talked about what happened when I went home to deal with my family. I discussed everything but the circumstances surrounding my mother's death.

I told her funny anecdotes about the funeral and how one of my mom's first cousins almost overturned the casket while attempting to kiss my mother and how another cousin decided that she wanted to sing "His Eye is on the Sparrow," but she could not sing, nor did she know the words to the song. So she made up the words for the entire song. For the main chorus, she sang, "I sings cuz I'm happy. I sings cuz I can. His eyes bees on the sparrows, so I knows he sees me." She laughed hard but told me that she did not believe me. I had Poo Man e-mail me the performance. Lisa laughed so hard while viewing it that tears rolled down her face.

After the third bottle of champagne, Lisa and I were making out hot and heavy. The next thing I knew, she had put a condom on me, and we were on the living room floor, butt naked, having wild sex. For the first time, I was having sex that did not include putting my dick in a man's ass. It felt different. And although I did not cum, I was not that bad. We must have done every style of fucking imaginable until her roommate came through the door. She gasped and said, "Oops! My bad." She covered her eyes and ran into her room.

Lisa and I just stopped and laughed. We grabbed our clothes that were spread out all over the living room and went into her room. Once we were there, I told her that I had some homework to do for my early class tomorrow, so I would be going to the bathroom to clean up and dress. She looked at me innocently and asked, "Ah, no round three?"

Instead of telling her that she was lucky to have had a round one, I kissed her and said, "Yeah, we will have to pick up where we left off later."

Once in the bathroom, I began thinking about our relationship. I liked Lisa a lot, but I knew it was not a love connection. I would have to think of a way to break it off with her. It was not fair to her to lead her on and have her believe that we could be a normal couple. After all, I had to get drunk just to get the desire to have sex with her. Lisa could have any man that she wanted. She had an energy that automatically attracted people to her. She deserved to be happy. I decided that I did not want her to think I just wanted to hit it and quit it, so I would wait a little while before I had that discussion with her.

On opening night of the season, I had a school breaking-record performance. After the game, I decided I would go to Lisa's to discuss our relationship. Lisa had missed the game because she told me that she had an important article to publish for the newspaper with a deadline for early the next week. Although the entire team went out to celebrate, I made my way to Lisa's, rehearsing what I would say to her along the way.

I arrived and nervously walked to the door. I knocked on the door, and it opened. Before I could call out Lisa's name, she came running out of her bedroom, giggling wearing a slinky red negligee with two empty champagne glasses. She stopped dead in her tracks, gasped, and dropped the glasses on the floor. I looked at her, shook my head, and then left.

Lisa called my phone several times, but I decided not to answer. I could not believe she was cheating on me. Yeah, I'd held out for a while and was going to break up with her, but she did not know that. I was faithful to her during our relationship and thought that she was faithful to me, too. What really upset me was that she decided to cheat on me when I was experiencing the most difficult time in my life. Despite me having to continue on with my life, school, and basketball, I was having a difficult time accepting my mother's death. I knew that, from here on out, it would be difficult for me to ever trust another woman again.

I really did not have time for a relationship anyway. I was more interested in getting my team to the championship game. We were a long way from the road to the championship, but this was the time to excel because March Madness would be here before we realized it. Although we practiced during the Christmas break, we were let out for a few days to be with our families. I had no motivation to go to Beaumont since my mother was gone. I decided that I would spend time with my aunt and Poo Man. I arrived in Houston to find out that Poo Man had moved out of his mom's. I spent five days of non-stop partying in Houston with Poo Man and his "freaks," as he called them.

I became an expert at drinking, while also keeping my wits enough to fight off Poo Man's freaks. I did not want to get caught up again in another Vernita situation, condom or no condom. Although the girls in Houston did not know who I was, some of them were only looking to ride the gravy train. My teammates labeled girls like that "bloodsuckers." Bloodsuckers were not only limited to hoodrats; they could also be the females who went to college just to find a husband to take care of them for the rest of their lives. One of the reasons I liked Lisa was because she was so independent; you knew she did not need or want a man to take care of her.

After break, our game schedule became more intense. I felt that I had to give everything I had to my team to take them to the next level. But I had a conflict between basketball and school. I had to decrease my time spent studying, which was contrary to why I was going to school. I was only playing basketball to get my free education to become a psychiatrist, but basketball was taking up all of my time. However, I knew that if we were going to win the ring, my interests could not be divided. It became clear to me that I was expected to put the team before anything or anyone else.

Chapter 9

I'm still not certain how things work in the universe or what God's exact plans are for us. During my first year of college, I don't understand how I was successful in all things. We won the ring, and my GPA was above a 4.0. Looking back, I knew that my mother was the most important person in my life. There was no way I could have had a balance between all of the things that were important to me and still reach my goals. I wondered whether God took my mother away from me so that I could achieve these things. If this was the case, I would have given everything back to have my mother here with me again.

I don't know at what point it happened, but probably during one of my drinking binges, I realized that I could do more good with money, than I could do by trying to reach kids individually to make a real difference in their lives. I decided to give up my pursuit of becoming a child psychiatrist and declare my eligibility for the NBA draft. After this announcement, my life went out of control. I began to get calls from agents, attorneys, marketing representatives, the news media, long lost cousins, and my dad. Or I should say, the man that provided the sperm in order for me to be conceived.

After much contemplation and advice from former teammates, I decided to hire an agent/attorney who had multi-faceted expertise in a variety of law specialties. Corbin O'Conner specialized in family law, criminal law, torts law, contract law, and sports and entertainment law. In addition to making certain I received the best contracts and endorsements, I figured, if I got in trouble for any reason, Corbin could hook me up. But most importantly, I wanted him to negotiate a contract with my sperm donor to get him out of my life permanently.

There was no reason for me to bond with him or anyone related to him after nineteen years of no contact. He did not even send condolences after my mother died. My attorney drew up a contract that included a "no contact" clause or he would forfeit the five million dollars' payable to him over the next twenty-five years. Considering the $120,000,000 four year-contract I signed with the Birmingham Slammers, I thought that was a good price to pay to get rid of scum.

I decided that I wanted to do things differently for my NBA career, and one of the first things I did was cut off my signature locks. When my grandmother first saw me without my locks, she declared loudly, "Boy, 'bout time you made yourself look like a man, instead of a girl."

I responded, "Well, Magrand, why don't you tell me how you really feel?"

My grandmother decided that she did not want to be called Grandma, so she changed it around to Magrand. This was fitting because everything my grandmother did was backwards. As a matter of fact, that is the way I felt about most of my relatives in Beaumont. But I had decided to stay at my mom's house to spend time with my family because I knew that is what my mom would have liked.

After leaving her family at an early age, she felt that spending time with family was important, and I wanted to make sure I honored her wishes. By the third day of dealing with uncles who thought they would play a father role to me at nineteen, male cousins with baby mama drama, female cousins who thought welfare was a way of life and that I should hook them up with a few bucks, and people who called themselves my friends from high school that I didn't ever remember speaking with, I had to escape to Houston.

I knew that my time in Houston would also be limited because my aunt wanted to feed me all day, while Poo Man wanted me to party with him all night. I had to get in shape for pre-season. I was entering a whole new world. My contract was one of the highest rookie contracts in NBA history, not counting the number of endorsements I had from major companies. I had to become more disciplined with my life, and that included everything, from what I ate to what I drank. I had been drinking heavily ever since high school, and

I noticed that that during my drinking binges, I did not use my best judgment.

I decided to spend most of my time exercising and practicing my skills on the court. I knew that in Houston, I would face worthy opponents. By this time, many of the people in the Ward knew who I was. Every time I went to the court, plenty of guys would show up just to prove their skills. Actually, I was impressed with the skills that many of them possessed. But for completing high school, some of them probably could have made it to the NBA.

One day while playing in the Ward, she showed up out of nowhere. I was already stricken by her beauty, but she balled like no woman I had ever seen. I could not concentrate on the game once she stepped on the court. I don't know exactly what it was, but I was completely mesmerized by her presence.

She had a toughness about her, but she still had beauty and grace. She had me so shaken that she actually stole the ball right out of my hands. My teammates started talking a lot of shit after that happened. I could tell by her comments that she did not know who I was. And that attracted me to her even more. I could not wait for the game to end to find out more about this intriguing girl who reminded me of Pocahontas.

I approached her and attempted to introduce myself, but she was sort of standoffish. She'd put down my game and gave me the cold shoulder. Her attitude turned me on even more. I had never quite experienced this type of attitude from anyone. The one thing that I knew was that I had to get to know this girl named Porchia before I left for Birmingham.

She walked up with Poo Man, so I knew he would give me the scoop on what I needed to know or do to penetrate her hard shell. After she left, the guys started talking about how they would love to get some of that. Poo Man became defensive and told them that Porchia would not give them the time of day.

I could see Poo Man was getting upset by the conversation, so although I wanted to play one more game, I gave everybody love and grabbed Poo Man and said, "Let's go see what Moms cooked today."

That was my way of diffusing the situation and getting some time with Poo Man to gently ease out information from him about Porchia. I started asking him simple questions like how did he know Porchia?

He looked at me and said, "Mane, not you, too! Porchia ain't that type."

"What type are you talking about?"

"Mane, don't play me. Like all those hos you used to messin' with."

"Poo, it ain't even like that."

"Then what is it like, mane?"

"I have a genuine interest in getting to know her."

"Yeah, whateva. Probably a genuine interest in gettin' between her legs."

"Poo, what you like her or something?"

"Nah, mane. That's my girl. I ain't gonna let no one mess her over."

"I swear to you Poo Man, I don't have any bad intentions toward her. I like her 'cause she seems to not know who I am."

"She doesn't. She asked about who you were, and I told her you were my li'l cuz."

I smiled after he said that. I knew I would have to turn on my magic to get Porchia to fall for me as I had fallen for her. I never believed in love at first sight, but I knew I wanted her to be part of my life. At the same time, I could not let Poo Man know how I was feeling because he would think I was a "sucka." It was even more troubling because I wanted to know every part of Porchia, not only her mind, but her body. I was feigning to have sex with her. That was a feeling that I had never experienced before with a female. How could all of this happen on a basketball court? This took *Love and Basketball* to a whole different level.

Poo Man told me that Porchia was a star basketball player at Yates, which I already knew by the way she handled herself on the court. Additionally, she was an honor roll student who was well-respected by everyone, including her teachers. However, Porchia was also known to have a short-fuse and would cuss out anyone she felt disrespected her.

When he said that, I felt an erection. All of the feelings I was experiencing were new to me. When Poo Man and I arrived at his mom's, Aunt Verdie's, I put in motion a plan to get Porchia's number. After we ate, I told Aunt Verdie and Poo Man that I was tired and needed to rest. Poo Man was also ready to go to his house, so we left.

After getting back to the house, I knew Poo Man would get into his games. He would get so engrossed in his games that the house could have burned down, and he would not have noticed. I took the opportunity to slip his phone off the coffee table and take it to the bathroom. Once I got in the bathroom, I scrolled through his list to find Porchia's number and saw no one named Porchia.

He had a few nicknames like Swallower, Slobber, and Deep Throat. I knew that, by the way he protected Porchia, he would never have her under one of those degrading names. However, the one name that stood out to me was "Shorty." I knew that, when Poo Man used this name, it was an endearing name for a female. I took a chance that this was Porchia, so I put the name "Pocahontas" and the number listed for Shorty in my phone. I then went back, and Poo Man was still caught up in his game. I slipped the phone back on the coffee table and sat back thinking about how best to approach Pocahontas. I fell asleep on the sofa thinking about her.

When I woke up, I had a strong desire to call Porchia. I knew my approach would have to be clever in order to get her to talk. If I thought about it too long, I knew I would bow out, so I just dialed the number, hoping that I had chosen the right one. I told myself, if it was not the correct number, it was not meant to be. My hand began sweating, and my heart rate increased when I heard her say, "Hello."

I called her Pocahontas, so she would immediately know who it was, and if she was not interested, she would let me know right away. She played the hard-girl role, but I could tell by the conversation that she was interested. I did not want to push it, so instead of asking her out on a date, I asked if she wanted to play a one-on-one game of basketball. By the time we hung up, I was gloating because I could feel our connection through the phone. I knew that one day, Pocahontas would be all mine.

Chapter 10

Poo Man and I had our first fight since we were children. He pretty much threatened to kill me if I did anything to hurt Porchia. He also confronted me about how I got her number. I confided in Poo Man about my real feelings for Porchia. I attempted to ask him questions about Porchia, and he let me know that anything I wanted to know about Porchia, I would have to find out for myself. I asked Poo Man if he liked Porchia beyond friends, and he told me that she would never give him the time of day. I don't know what I would have done if he said he liked Porchia beyond friends because I felt that we were destined to be together.

I waited for Porchia at the park, but she did not show. I called her and found out that she'd had an emergency with her aunt. She sounded upset, and I wanted to make certain I was there to help her. I must have broken every traffic law that existed to get to her. When I pulled up, she was standing there with a security guard and a lady that looked as if she could have been Porchia's older sister.

The lady, who had more attitude than Porchia, was Porchia's cousin named Mystery. Mystery looked me up and down, turned up her nose, and then told me that she would not take a ride from a drug dealer. She was comical, and I would have found her very entertaining if Porchia didn't look so upset.

Although our first date was at a hospital, it did not matter. I would have spent time with her at a graveyard, if it was necessary. During our date, I spent my time keeping Porchia from cussing out her aunt's pastor and preventing her from attempting to beat down Mystery. Her rash personality turned me on even more than her moves on the court. I could not wait to get to know Porchia from head-to-toe.

I knew it was irrational, but I needed some additional time to spend with Porchia because I wanted to be her support system. I could not leave Porchia at a time like this because I could tell, by the interaction between her and her cousin, that they had a strained relationship. And it was even more evident that Porchia relied heavily on her aunt for support, much as I had relied on my mother for mine. The feeling of being all alone is something that a person should not have to experience.

I knew that I would have to pull some strings to get additional time away from my team. I called Corbin, and he told me he would take care of everything, but then Corbin called me back to inform me that the team insisted that I report on the agreed upon date. I called and personally spoke to the manager of player relations. This was the first time I realized that there was a lot of bureaucracy involved with the NBA. I was able to get an additional two days off before having to leave for Birmingham.

The truth of the matter was, I also needed the additional time. I was not certain I had made the right decision to leave college for the NBA. My life seemed to be transitioning to something that I was unfamiliar with. I wanted to return to the simple days of high school and my times of partying in college. But more than anything, I wanted Porchia to realize that I was serious about getting to know her better.

During my brief visit, I bonded with Porchia's Aunt Hattie. She was a delightful woman, and very much the opposite of my grandmother. She met no strangers and made me feel like I was part of the family immediately. I made arrangements for Aunt Hattie to be taken care of prior to leaving Houston. I hired a nurse to be there for her during her recovery period. Porchia was not happy about my actions and let me know that she did not appreciate me getting into her business.

Porchia was even more upset when she found out that I was Tyrese Gamble and not Ty, the guy she beat on the court. I knew it would be difficult to penetrate the hard exterior that Pocahontas liked to project to the world, but I would die trying. I tried to get information from Poo Man about what I could do to soften Porchia's heart, but he told me I was on my own. I don't ever recall being so enamored by a person, and I was not certain what to do to get her attention. She made me feel as if I was in junior high school again, trying to figure out the way to a girl's vagina.

In the midst of all of the confusion about going to the NBA and my feelings for Porchia, I received an unexpected call. I answered and heard, "Hey, man."

The voice sounded familiar, but I could not quite place the voice. I said, "Yeah, who dis?"

"Oh, I see. You got a NBA contract and forgot all about me?"

I then realized it was Clayton. "What up, bro? I have not heard from you in a grip."

"Well, I am in town and thought we could get together," Clayton said.

"Ah, man. I am in Houston and headed to B-ham, bro. I am going to have to catch you another time."

"Bet. I may be able to come to Birmingham to see you."

"I will probably be spending a lot of time practicing. But hit me up."

"Okay. Nice talking with you," Clayton said, sounding deflated.

"Stay in touch, bro." I hung up the phone knowing that he was the last person I wanted to see. I had put that life all behind me. Porchia was the only person that occupied my thoughts and, hopefully soon, my body.

Poo Man, knowing that I was headed out, planned a party for me with a lot of his folks. I looked around and was disappointed to find out that Porchia was not there.

I pulled Poo Man aside and said, "So why did you not invite Porchia?"

"Mane, Porchia would not come to nothing like this."

"What do you mean?"

"Porchia is into nothing but basketball and school. She ain't got time for bullshit. Mane, these hos right here ready to give you everything you want."

"Yeah, and things I don't want, like some type of disease."

"You were not saying that shit before you got that contract."

"Poo Man, don't go acting like I'm being brand new with you. You know me better than that!"

"Mane, I just think you need to do you. Let Porchia do her."

"Look, Poo Man, I ain't never met someone that made me feel the way I feel about Porchia."

"You just met her mane!"

"I know. It may not make no sense. But it is like love at first sight for me. I want Porchia to be a part of my life."

"Mane, you talkin' that drunk talk. You gonna be in the NBA; you gonna have all kind of hos throwing pussy at you."

"I don't know why I am talking to you about this," I said and walked out of the house.

I walked to the park where I first met Porchia and sat on the bench and got caught up in my thoughts. All I could do was think about Porchia — how her hair smelled, how she rolled her eyes, how she walked, how she spoke — until I was surrounded by a group of thugs. They looked me up and down for a minute until one got up in my face and asked, "What you doing here, busta?"

Another one said, "Hold on, mane. That is Tyrese Gamble."

"Oh, shit! You are right. Sorry, folk."

I got up and said, "No problem. Just thinking about my game."

"Make us proud, folk. Good luck with the Slammers," the little one who was all up in my face said.

"No doubt. Stay up," I said while chucking deuces.

I walked out of the park thinking about how that could have gone all bad.

I decided to go to my aunt's because I did not want to deal with Poo Man and his crew. My aunt instinctively knew that something was wrong and asked me what had happened between me and Poo Man. I just told her that I was not in the mood for partying and needed time to regroup before leaving for Birmingham.

Aunt Verdie tried to play the role of mama and gave me a pep talk about entering into the NBA. She told me to have confidence in myself and to keep my trust in God. And she assured me that she would be there if I needed anything as she had promised my mother on her death bed. I thanked Aunt Verdie for the talk and went to the room. I decided to call Porchia. She was being her usual standoffish self. After hanging up with Porchia, I went to bed with a heavy heart and tears in

my eyes. How I wished that my mother could be here.
I knew she could help me sort out my feelings.

Chapter 11

The trip to Birmingham was gruesome. From the time I got off the plane, I felt I had made the biggest mistake of my life. I was greeted at the airport by a driver who took me straight to our practice facility. I was immediately reprimanded for walking into the facility wearing jeans and a T-shirt. I was informed by the assistant practice manager that the organization was run like a Fortune 500 corporation. He told me that I was part of the C-Suite and was expected to show up in appropriate attire.

General Roach, as he called himself, told me that the first order of attention each day would be a meeting where we discussed the day's schedule and what was expected from the players and supporting staff. He proceeded to hand me a two-hundred-page book of rules and regulations for the Birmingham Slammer Organization and told me that I would be tested on the content. I wanted to ask him whether I was getting punked, but his demeanor screamed to me that he was dead serious.

He went on to tell me that the players were in practice, and he did not want to interrupt them, but I was expected to show up on time tomorrow, so I could get an appropriate introduction to the team. He also told me that I was expected to take the test on the rules and regulations tomorrow. He also informed me that I would be fined $5,000 for each minute that I was late for either practice or a game. He then asked me to tear a sheet from the back of the rules and regulations book and sign and date that I had received the rules. I felt that I should have, also, saluted him and shouted, "Yes, sir!"

General Roach then passed me on to the facilities manager, who had a demeanor that was much calmer than the General's. He gave me a tour of our practice facility, which included the shower, the weight room, the locker room, the conference room, and the coaches' offices. We then took a shuttle to the arena, and he showed me all of the facilities within the arena. I was impressed, yet intimidated by the size of the arena. It reminded me of a little city. I had been to several arenas, but this place seemed humongous compared to the places that I had previously seen. Birmingham had gone out of it way to build this 30,000 seating capacity arena.

Upon my return to the practice facility, I was introduced to several coaches and other managers who managed things I can't even remember. The facility manager had already informed me that the four most important people for me to get to know were the general manager, who took a hands-on approach with the team; the player-development coach, who would make certain I developed into an A-1 player for the team; the equipment coach, who would make certain I had everything I needed for the games; and the union representative leader of the team, because there may be times when I would need assistance working through the bureaucracy. I knew I was "a long ways" away from high school basketball, where I had excelled and was considered "Da Man," and did not need anyone or anything to help me succeed.

I left Houston without saying bye to Poo Man, so he called me a few days later to make certain that we were cool. I told him we would always be cool and that he would always be my brother. He apologized for being so hard on me about Porchia and told me that he thought that we would make a good couple. The call from Poo Man built up the confidence that I was lacking at that time. I remembered when I met the guys who I played with in college, we all were like family. I was always taught that there was no "I" in team, but with the Slammers, I felt like there were a lot of "I's" coming together, trying to make something happen.

I spent a lot of time talking with Coc, the name I gave Corbin, about getting me out of the contract. When I finally got it through my head that I would be playing with the Slammers, I had to find a way to make it work. I began interacting with the players on a personal level to bring us together as a team. The shooting guard and the point guard did not care for each other. The center thought the strong forward was trying to take on his role. The sixth man thought that he should be a starter. During this time of trying to be

Mr. Social and bring the team together, the shooting guard, Raheem Shivers, befriended me. We found ourselves doing a lot of activities outside of practice.

Raheem helped me find a real estate agent, personal finance manager, and a life coach who was an ex-pro basketball player. I found all of this really helpful to me. Once I closed on the house, I told Raheem that I wanted to make dinner for him and his wife, Jinn. When Jinn found out my family was originally from Louisiana, she asked me if I knew how to make gumbo. When I told her that was literally the only dish I knew how to cook, she sounded excited. So to show my appreciation to them, I decided to cook them a gumbo.

Raheem showed up alone, carrying two bottles of wine. He entered saying, "I did not know if red or white wine went with gumbo, so I brought both."

When I asked him where Jinn was, he told me she was under the weather but insisted that he come and take her some gumbo back home.

I welcomed Raheem to sit down at the bar while I dropped the seafood into the gumbo. He refused and said that he was cool and took a seat at the counter in the kitchen. I asked him if he was hungry, and he told me he could wait for the final dish. In the meantime, he asked me whether I wanted him to open up a bottle of wine, and I told him sure. He opened the white wine which was a Riesling. We drank and talked about what was going on with the team.

Once the gumbo was ready, I handed him a bowl and told him to help himself. I asked him whether he wanted something else to drink, and he asked me if I had something stronger than wine. I told him to go check out the liquor display, and he came back with the Gran Patrón Platinum. I thought, *That is what you get for letting a nicca choose.* I had been saving that Patrón for some unknown special occasion, but I knew I could always afford another bottle. Plus, I was really appreciative for what he had done for me.

We took a shot before we ate our gumbo, and I was not certain how many shots we took after we ate our gumbo. But we ended up butt-naked on the kitchen floor. I realized that Raheem must have come prepared for the occasion because he had condoms ready for the event. I asked him how he knew that I would have sex with him. He told me that he did not know, but he knew exactly what he wanted. I had not had sex since I'd had sex with Lisa, so the dick was good. It reminded me of the times I'd had with Clayton. But as good as the sex was, all I could think about was that I was cheating on Porchia. It was crazy because the last time we talked she had pretty much dismissed me.

Before Raheem left, he said that he had no regrets and that he hoped that I had none either. I told him that I hoped that this did not mess up the relationship that we had on the court. He assured me that he could separate the two and that everything would be cool. The minute he left, I started thinking about what I could do to make sure it never happened again.

But I also could not stop thinking about how good it felt, and how he reawakened something in me that had been dormant for a while. To push those thoughts out of my head, I called Porchia. I was not happy that she did not answer my call, so I took a hot shower to wash away the thoughts of me and Raheem having hot sex.

The next day at practice, I did not make eye contact with Raheem at all. When we went to take a shower, he stopped and looked at me and said, "Is everything okay?"

I just nodded my head and kept on showering. Some of the guys said they were going to grab something to eat. I had worked so hard at getting us together as a team, and I felt what I had done with Raheem might cause a division again because I turned them down on their invitation.

Within a few minutes of arriving home, my doorbell rang. I checked my security cameras and saw that it was Raheem. I thought about not answering the door but knew that we had to work together. When I opened the door, Raheem unbuttoned my pants, pulled them down, bent me over, and gave it to me right at the door. After he finished, he cleaned up and said, "Until next time," and walked out of the door.

Chapter 12

I finally got in touch with Porchia, and I knew right away something was wrong. I found out that her best friend, Chanti, was killed in a drive-by shooting. She sounded very distraught, and I wanted to get to her as quickly as possible. Although Porchia told me that she did not want me to come, I decided to speak with the manager of team relations, Tom Oreck, and told him that my cousin was killed and that my aunt was having a difficult time. He told me that I should work it out with my coaches to see if they were in agreement that I could have a little time off.

I decided to run it by my life coach, and he explained to me that, unless it was an immediate family member, it would be frowned upon if I took off time to go to a relative's funeral. I told Sweezy to keep an eye on her, and if she was having too difficult of a time, I would leave regardless of what anyone here said. Porchia was more important to me than any type of fine they might give me for missing practice. After Poo Man said Porchia was taking it hard, I decided that I would definitely be there to support Porchia during the service. I decided to do a turnaround trip, so I would not miss any practice.

****

The surprise visit to Porchia proved to be very profitable. I knew that I had penetrated Porchia's hard shell because she opened up to me. It felt great just having her near me in bed all night, although nothing happened because Porchia was drunk. I wanted our first experience to be enjoyable and memorable for both of us.

While in Houston, I received several calls from Raheem, none of which I answered. On one call, he cussed me out and told me I did not know who I was messing with. He also said that I better not be with no other nicca. I thought, *This is odd behavior for a married man.* But I just dismissed the call because I was exactly with who I wanted to be with, and Raheem nor anyone else would ever come between me and Porchia.

Once I returned to Birmingham, I found out that Porchia did not accept the gift that I had picked out for her. But she made up for that by verbalizing that we were in a relationship during a phone conversation. I was so excited when Porchia, for the first time, picked up the phone to call me. However, it was odd that she had called to tell me about a friend that was being sexually abused by a relative. This took me back to what Rico had done to me. It also made me wonder about why I felt I could love Porchia, while also having a strong desire to be with Raheem. After the conversation with Porchia, I decided that I would cut off my "relationship" with Raheem.

The only thoughts that possessed my mind were about Porchia and being there for the team as a key player. However, Raheem had his own agenda. Raheem sweated me until I agreed to meet him at a neutral place to talk. We met at an out of the way spot, but were recognized by several of the patrons. I basically told Raheem that it was over and that I did not want anything but a teammate relationship. Raheem told me that no one just broke it off with him without consequences. I didn't know what that meant, but I got up from the table and left Raheem sitting there before the drinks came.

****

I was excited that Porchia was coming to visit me, and I wanted to make everything perfect for her. I wanted to impress her, so I hired an interior decorator to help me decorate my unfurnished rooms. Although Porchia was not attached to material things, I wanted to be on my A-game. I even purchased a white grand piano for the formal living room accompanied by white furniture. I got the game room together because I knew Porchia would enjoy playing the games and she liked shooting pool.

On the day that Porchia was supposed to arrive, Raheem came to my house demanding an explanation for why I was cutting him off. I'd heard about women doing this, but I was surprised to find him acting like a straight bitch. To get rid of him, I told him that a lot was going on back home and that I just needed time. He left me with only a little time to get ready for my girl. I wanted to make certain I greeted her properly and made her feel like royalty; I still needed to get the flowers and champagne. I wanted to make this an unforgettable weekend for her.

There was a lot going on in Porchia's life. She was offered a full academic scholarship at Georgetown, but it did not include playing basketball. Basketball was Porchia's love, so I could not imagine her being happy with going to school without the opportunity to play ball. But this weekend, I wanted us both to forget about our problems and concentrate on us. If it were up to me, we would be so absorbed in each other that what was happening in the outside world would not matter to either one of us.

The weekend turned out to be perfect. I catered to all of Porchia's needs, including making certain she was satisfied in bed. I found out that Porchia was a virgin, and I also felt like I was making love for the very first time. I was a little worried that I would not be able to perform since I had only had sex with a woman when I was drunk. But making love to Porchia was so different; it was unlike anything that I had ever experienced with a man or woman.

Porchia was my intoxicant because I could not get enough of her. I was ready to bend down on one knee and ask her to be in my life forever. I knew that Porchia would not agree and say it was premature. She still had her armor on and was concerned about getting hurt. She told me that was all that she had seen from relationships — people hurting each other. I knew that we could be different, if she only would give us a chance.

The day arrived for Porchia to leave, and I felt at a loss. Reality hit that I had a lot to deal with once she left. Raheem had called several times, but I had my ringer on silent. I was at a point that I felt uncomfortable going to practice. It affected how I interacted with the team, but I knew I would have to pull it together, so the Slammers would be successful. Since we were an expansion team, the NBA was not expecting a lot from us; despite the infighting, we expected a lot from each other. We wanted to be included in the post-season and worked very hard at being a worthy contender.

****

By the time we reached the halfway mark in the season, all of the major networks were talking about the Slammers. I got so much coverage on ESPN they started calling it TGSN, which stood for Ty Gamble's Sports Network. I was flattered by the coverage, but it made my life that much more difficult. Even under disguise, I could not go to the gas station without someone recognizing me. I hired a staff to do all of my errands. I even hired a full-time driver who was really helpful with ensuring that I made all of my appointments. I had a barber, a massage therapist, and a personal shopper that frequented my house as well.

Despite my busy schedule, I stayed in close contact with Porchia as often as possible. I wanted her to know that she was the most important person in my life. I fought off groupies on a daily basis. Although the team and I played well on the court, none of us were exceptionally close. I was able to keep my personal life out of the limelight. I was also able to keep Raheem at a distance. I figured he must have found someone else to keep him satisfied.

I wanted Porchia to have a normal high school life; not a life where she was constantly harassed by the media. I was approached by a network that wanted to do a reality show about NBA girlfriends. They asked whether or not I was in a relationship. I told them that I was in a relationship with basketball, and I did not have time for anything or anyone else. That seemed to work well until All-Star Weekend.

Our relationship was on blast in Detroit during All-Star Weekend. Photographers caught us going to and leaving spots together, hand-in-hand. She was reported as being Ty Gamble's under-aged girlfriend who had a love for basketball as much as he did. That became a story for a while, but Porchia dealt with it eloquently. She did not allow the media to affect anything that she did or did not do.

Raheem had a totally different reaction to finding out about Porchia. He threatened several times to let Porchia know what was going on between us. I figured it was all talk because he would not want Jinn to know that he was more interested in men's asses than women's pussies. Raheem went out of his way to pretend to be a womanizer, making sure he got caught with as many females as possible in compromising positions, while calling me, telling me that all he could think about was my ass. However, he eased up off me a little when I found him after-hours in the shower sucking one of the assistant coaches' dicks. After that occasion, the assistant coach never looked me in the eye. That experience made me wonder how many guys in the NBA were actually on the down low, and even more importantly, how many were Raheem doing?

Chapter 13

Things were going well for the Slammers, and my name was being thrown around for the leading nomination for Rookie of the Year. I did not see Porchia as often as I would have liked, but our relationship was getting stronger every day. I set up Porchia to be able to see me anytime she wanted. There were two people that had full access to my home, Poo Man and Porchia. Poo Man came up a couple of times, but said that Birmingham was too slow for him.

Poo Man really did not like Birmingham, because when he came up, there were a lot of groupies looking for ballers. They flocked to Birmingham because it was the only city in Alabama that had a professional team. If not in Birmingham, the groupies were scoping out Montgomery for future NFL players from Alabama State.

We had nicknames for all the groupies that were even known by the visiting teams. After the games, we usually partied with our opponents and the same ol' groupies. I made some good friends during All-Star Weekend and actually had more "friends" from other teams than friends who were on my team. I probably felt more comfortable with them because none of them knew my secret. It also became apparent to me how much staging was done for basketball teams that were supposed to be rivals. I partied with my rivals all the time, and we kept in touch between games. But the media routinely made mountains out of mole hills for the sake of sensation and ratings.

****

One morning Jinn called me crying, asking me whether I had seen Raheem because he had not come home all night. I told her the last time I had seen Raheem was at the game, and I was sorry that I could not help her. She told me that he often said that he spent the night at my house because he was too drunk to drive. I did not want to become involved in their problems, so I told her that sometimes he did. The truth was that I had not seen Raheem in a while. I figured that he'd found some other ass that he liked. Perhaps the assistant coach was filling that bill.

One night the team went out, and we all had too much to drink. I stopped drinking and driving because professional sports players were being targeted for DUIs. One time there was a big deal about spousal/partner abuse, but the focused had now changed to drinking and driving after three professional players were caught driving under the influence. For the first DUI offense, the penalty was a twelve-game suspension. Raheem always drove, but he was fucked up, so he asked me whether my driver could take him home. I was a little hesitant about driving him home, but I thought, as a teammate, it was the right thing to do.

Raheem fell out in the car, and we could not wake him up for him to give us directions or the address to his house. I called Jinn to get their address, but she did not answer. I left a message for her to call me. Because I had nowhere to take him, I told the driver to drive us home. I walked Raheem to one of my guest rooms, threw him down on the bed, and took off his shoes.

I figured, once he sobered up, my driver could drive him to his house. In the meantime, I went to my room and called Porchia, but her phone went straight to voicemail. So I left her a message telling her that I was thinking about her and that I loved her. I drifted off to sleep with thoughts of Porchia on my mind.

When I woke up the next morning, I was startled to find Raheem butt naked, lying next to me, and smiling.

I jumped up and said, "What the fuck are you doing in my bed man?"

"Don't get all brand new on me son. You know how we do it."

"Nah, Raheem. That shit is through."

"I know you want me as bad as I want you."

When I saw him staring at my dick that was protruding through my shorts, I defensively said, "I ain't feeling you like that."

"Well, your dick is saying otherwise," he said with a devilish smirk on his face.

Before I knew it, he had my dick in his mouth and was sucking it like the world was coming to an end. I was speechless. I stood there until he looked at me and said, "Now get in this bed and let me give you what you want."

I was under his spell as I assumed the doggy-style position. He searched his pants for a condom while I anxiously waited for him to enter me. He teased me for about five minutes before penetrating me. I immediately orgasmed. He then started banging me at a rapid pace. As I moaned, he said, "Give it all to daddy."

I raised up my ass, so he could put all of him in me, and at that moment, the door opened, and I heard, "Surprise, baby!"

Chapter 14

If I had to choose the moment when I knew that it had all gone bad, it was at that moment when Porchia caught me ass-up with Raheem. There was nothing I could say to justify what she had witnessed. If she had caught me with another woman, I think we might have had a chance, but I saw all chances for happiness with her vanish right in front of me when she ran out of the room. I attempted to run after her, but she was down the stairs before I could even put on my pants.

If that was not enough, by the time I got outside, Porchia was lying face down with blood streaming from her head, onto the street. I immediately started screaming, "Call 911!"

Porchia was lying lifeless in front of me, and I had killed her. Raheem came out asking what happened. I told him to get the fuck away from me.

A man came up and shouted, "Sorry! She came out of nowhere! I did not see her!"

"This is not a damn raceway! How fast were you going?" I asked hysterically.

"Not fast at all. Is she okay?"

"Does she look okay? Call 911!"

93

Although I thought Porchia was dead, I cradled her in my arms and told her that everything would be fine. And I told her that I was sorry for everything. Minutes later, the ambulance and police arrived on the scene. They immediately hauled Porchia away, and the police started asking me questions that I could not answer. I thought that instead of questioning me, they needed to arrest the driver. I lashed out at them by saying, "If this was a white woman lying here because a black man had hit her, y'all probably would have shot him in the back by now!"

The driver was visually shaken and began mumbling all sort of crazy things. I told the police I needed to get to the hospital and asked where Porchia was being taken. They told me that they needed all of my information before I left. I became irritated because I felt they were treating me like I was a criminal. I knew, for Porchia's sake, I needed to calm down and attempt to give the information that they requested. After cooperating with the officers, I got in my car and sped all the way to the hospital. When I arrived at the hospital, Raheem called me and asked me how was he supposed to get home. My response was, "Fuck you!" before pressing the end button.

I was immediately recognized by the hospital staff, and they promised to keep me apprised of Porchia's condition. It struck me, while pacing back and forth that Porchia's family did not know what happened. I had to get in touch with Aunt Hattie and Mystery to let them know what was going on.

I realized I did not have Aunt Hattie's number, but Mystery had called me not that long ago asking me whether Porchia and I were having protected sex. I thought it was odd for her cousin to be worried about whether Porchia and I were using condoms, but I assured her that we were and that I would never do anything to hurt Porchia. Now she was in the hospital in critical condition because of me.

I was caught up in my thoughts when the doctor came out and said that Porchia was unconscious and nonresponsive. He informed me that he was placing her in ICU because she would require constant monitoring. The doctor rambled on about something else, but it seemed that, in that moment, my heart stopped. I knew that I could never forgive myself if Porchia did not make it.

How am I going to face her family and tell them I am the reason for her death? How can I face myself knowing that I killed the person that I most loved in this world? I wondered. I'd only recently gained Porchia's trust, and now her trust in me was not worth a penny with a hole in it. I would gladly replace my life for hers. I wanted God to hear my prayers. I prayed silently, "Please, Lord, keep Porchia safe within your arms and return her to us."

The doctor looked at me and said, "Who is her next of kin? There may be some decisions that we need to make about her care."

I told the doctor that I would call her family as soon as possible. He looked at me and said, "The time is now. If you have any other questions, I have written my contact information on the board in Porchia's room."

"Doctor, can I go see her?"

"Sure. She is unconscious. But I think she needs to be surrounded by people who love her. That may bring her back."

When he said that, I thought, *I am probably the last person she wants to come back to.*

****

Before calling Mystery, I wanted to make certain I called the airline to coordinate flight plans, pay for a hotel, and get them transportation from the airport to the hospital. Once I made those plans, I called Mystery. She sounded confused and flustered, but said they would get here as soon as possible. I gave her the flight information and told her that I had purchased first-class tickets, so they could change it to leave at a time that was convenient for them.

After speaking with Mystery, I went to Porchia's room. It reminded me of when I walked into my mother's room for the last time. I stopped dead in my tracks before entering the room. I said a quick prayer to God and asked Him again to bring Porchia back to us. When I walked in the room, I saw that her face was bruised and swollen. Tears immediately welled up in my eyes. I was responsible for all of this. *How could I hurt someone that I love so much?* I wondered.

I walked over to Porchia and told her that I was sorry. I told her that I loved her. I told her that I would always be there for her, if she would just come back. I told her that she never had to worry about me cheating on her again. I was pouring out my heart to her when a nurse came in and told me that she needed to check her vitals. I asked her whether she needed me to step out, and she told me I could stay. It seemed like something was wrong with Porchia's blood pressure reading because she took it several times. She looked at me and said, "I will have to consult with the doctor. Her blood pressure is extremely low."

The nurse came back and put something into Porchia's IV and said, "This should help increase her blood pressure."

I asked whether Porchia could hear us, and she said, "I am not certain. But you should speak to her as if she hears you." I was looking at Porchia, and it looked like she blinked her eyes. I shouted, "I think she blinked!"

"Yes, she may have some involuntary movements. But that does not mean she is necessarily conscious."

I looked at the nurse and asked her, "Do you believe in God?"

She responded, "Yes, I do."

"Do you mind joining me in a prayer for Porchia?"

She smiled and said, "It would be my pleasure."

I led us in a short prayer, asking God for Porchia's full and complete recovery. When I finished, the nurse responded loudly, "Amen! God had to hear that heart-felt prayer."

I smiled, and she grabbed my hand and said, "She will come back," then walked out of the room.

I went and sat next to Porchia and said, "Pocahontas, I promise you that I will spend the rest of my life making this up to you. Just come back. Although I don't deserve you, I can't live without you." Tears started rolling from my eyes, and I could not control them. I must have sat there for hours holding her hand, crying, and praying. My phone rang, and it was Tom Oreck. I felt that we had gotten to know each other really well because I kept having personal issues since I'd started my pro career.

"Hey, Tom."

"Hey there, rookie. You missed practiced today."

"Yeah, I am sorry, but my girlfriend is in critical condition. She was hit by a car."

"Yeah, Raheem informed Coach. I am calling you to let you know your fine has been waived. But we will need you to show up for the game. Please show up to practice with the team."

"Bet. Thanks, Tom."

"No problem. Take care."

I guess Raheem was good for something. I had completely forgotten about practice, basketball, and the team. I was glad that the organization seemed to be understanding. But at this point, I did not care if they understood or not. I could not leave Porchia alone. I was the reason that she was in this condition. I received a couple of other calls from team members who had met Porchia during All-Star Weekend. They called to give me their well-wishes and prayers for a speedy recovery. It felt good to know that they cared.

Chapter 15

I met Aunt Hattie and Mystery in the lobby. I wanted to give them an update on Porchia's condition. Mystery, who normally looked stunning, looked as if she had not slept in days, and Aunt Hattie was a complete wreck. I told them that I had booked a hotel for them if they wanted to go freshen up. Both refused and said they wanted to see Porchia right away.

I led them up to Porchia's room but asked both of them if we could pray before going into the room. Aunt Hattie was a God-loving/God-fearing woman, so I knew that God would hear her prayer. But when we grabbed hands, words just started coming out of my mouth. This was the first time this had happened to me. I was not in charge of what was going on or being said. Aunt Hattie looked at me and said, "That was a great prayer, baby. I know God heard you." We then all walked into Porchia's room.

When she saw Porchia, Mystery screamed, "No, my baby! My baby!"

"Hush, Mystery, with all of that drama!" Aunt Hattie snapped.

I stood there completely confused.

Mystery looked back at Aunt Hattie and said, "It is all my fault Aunt Hattie. I tried so hard to protect my baby, but all I did was end up killing her."

"Mystery, you need to have faith. Baby Girl ain't going nowhere. So start believing. Didn't you hear that boy's prayer? It will be answered!"

The more they carried on, the more confused I became. But eventually I began to realize that Mystery was Porchia's mother, not her cousin. Now it made sense. Porchia probably came to me because she was upset. She actually did not like Mystery and fought with her all the time. I could only imagine how Porchia felt running to me only to find me in bed with Raheem. I had to talk with Porchia. I convinced Mystery and Aunt Hattie to go get something to eat.

"Pocahontas, I am so sorry. You have experienced more pain than anyone should have to face. But if you come back, my whole life will be dedicated to making you do nothing but smile. Not out of obligation or because I feel totally responsible for what happened, but because I love you like I have never loved anyone. I didn't know how to love until I met you. I didn't think I could ever have any deep feelings for a person outside of my family, until I met you. You have brought out the best in me, and I need you to give me the opportunity to show you that I am the best man for you. Your mother and aunt are here now. They want to spend some time with you. I am going to my game but will return right after I finish. I love you now and will love you forever. I will be back Pocahontas. Please be up, so we can talk. I love you."

As I finished my talk, Mystery and Aunt Hattie returned. I kissed them both and told them I would be back as soon as possible. They both thanked me for being there for Porchia. What they both did not know was that I was the reason she was lying lifeless in that hospital bed.

I knew that I would never forgive myself if something happened. Before leaving, I had to let Mystery know that she was not at fault. I told her she did the best that she could do for Porchia, and one day, I knew that Porchia would understand. Mystery's eyes were red and swollen. She whimpered, "Thanks Ty for being here for her. She needs you more than ever now."

I left thinking about Mystery's words. I wondered whether I was actually good for her or really a deterrent to her waking up. She'd run to me for comfort, and I'd only brought her more pain. Even if Porchia forgave me, I was not certain that I could ever forgive myself.

I prayed to God again and asked Him to give me another opportunity to make it up to Porchia. I cried and told God that she had a lot to offer the world, and I knew it was not her time. All of my prayers were probably falling on deaf ears, since I was not worthy to ask anything of Him.

****

I made it to practice, but after practice, Coach pulled me aside and told me that he'd noticed my mind was not into the game. He told me he would start me for the first quarter, but he wanted me to fake an injury, so he could release me for the rest of the game. We were playing the team with the worst record in the NBA, and he told me he knew they could win the game without me.

So as Coach instructed, I came down weird on my ankle and was taken out of the game for the rest of the night. He later caught me in the locker room and told me he needed to speak with me privately. He told me that he could buy me time out of practice and the next three games, all of which were on the road, if I needed the additional time. I told Coach I would play it by ear and get back to him. He asked me to directly contact him and no one else. I thanked him, and he hugged me and told me to take care of myself and Porchia.

I went straight back to the hospital after the game. Porchia was still in the same condition, and Mystery and Aunt Hattie were right by her side. I walked in and immediately felt the love. I also felt that I was out of place, since I was the reason for Porchia being in that room. I told them I wanted to speak to the doctor to find out what the latest prognosis was.

I knew that, sometimes, there were unconventional treatments that could possibly bring a person out of a coma. When I spoke to the doctor, he assured me that the best thing we could do was be there for Porchia and pray. I started doubting whether I was the best thing for Porchia. At that moment, I decided that I would join my team on the road.

When I came back to the room, Aunt Hattie asked me what the doctor said. I told her the doctor assured me that everything was being done to provide Porchia with the best medical help. Aunt Hattie then looked at Mystery and said, "Come on, Mystery. Let's give Ty some time with Baby Girl."

Once they left the room, I grabbed Porchia's hand, "I know that I am the reason that you're not waking up. So I'm going to go away for a little while. I'm going to meet the team on the road. I pray that when I leave, you'll return to the family that need and love you so much. You should see Mystery. She is losing her mind. Pocahontas, I know that Mystery loves you more than you can ever imagine. And you know that you're Aunt Hattie's world. Her one and only Baby Girl," I paused and smiled.

My smile quickly vanished when I realized that perhaps she would never wake up. I continued by saying, "I know I'm the last person you probably want to hear this from, but I love you too. I'll spend the rest of my days trying to make up for what I did. Please come back to us."

Once Mystery and Aunt Hattie returned, I told them about my plans. Mystery said that they could handle it and wished me luck in my games. I kissed Aunt Hattie, and I could tell she seemed confused. It was like Aunt Hattie knew my thoughts without me speaking about it. She whispered, "Whatever happened. It was not your fault."

I smiled and said, "I love you Aunt Hattie. I will be back soon."

Upon leaving the hospital, I called Coach to let him know that I would be joining the team on the road. I was thankful that the press had not gotten a hold of the story about "Tyrese Gamble's girlfriend getting hit by a truck as she was leaving his house." I could only imagine the frenzy it would have caused and the twist they would put on the story. I probably would have joined the list of boyfriends and husbands who abused their significant others. The truth of the matter was, I had probably caused more harm to Porchia than any of the players who had been exposed for physical abuse.

Chapter 16

I called and spoke to Mystery as often as possible during my road trip. She informed me that there had not been a change in Porchia's condition. During one conversation, she told me that she thought we had lost her. She had an emotional breakdown over the phone. I did all I could do to comfort her. After the conversation, I knew I should have stayed in Birmingham to be there for her and Aunt Hattie. The minute I returned, I rushed to the hospital. While Aunt Hattie and I were talking about the games, Mystery shouted, "She is waking up!"

I ran, while Aunt Hattie waddled to the bed. Porchia's eyes were fluttering, so Aunt Hattie told Mystery to run and get the nurse.

Instead of the nurse coming, the doctor came in, smiling. He looked at us and said, "Can I have some time alone to examine the patient?"

I felt as if my heart was going to come out of my chest. I was so excited because I had started believing that she would never come back to us. We all walked out, and Aunt Hattie began doing her happy dance and saying, "Can't nobody do you like Jesus. Thank you Lawd for hearing our prayers!"

My emotions started flowing out-of-control, so much so, I wanted to break out into a full chorus with Aunt Hattie. Instead, I silently said my own personal prayer and thanked the Lord.

It had been almost two years since I'd lost the first woman that I ever loved. I didn't think I could live with myself if I lost the only other woman I'd ever loved, especially if I lost her because of something I'd done.

When the doctor finished examining Porchia, he came out and said, "She'll be okay. I want to conduct another MRI, but she's as sharp as a tack. She may have some memory loss, but she seems to be headed toward a full recovery. She will need her rest, so try not to tire her out. She may have a lot to say and want to do a lot of talking, but don't encourage her."

We all thanked the doctor and hurried back into the room where we found Porchia sitting up, looking confused. Aunt Hattie and Mystery rushed over to Porchia. They hugged and kissed her as I stood back, smiling. After about a ten-minute reunion between the three of them, Aunt Hattie suggested to Mystery that they give me and Porchia some private time. Aunt Hattie looked at Porchia and said, "Baby Girl, we will give you some time with Ty. We will be right outside if you need anything."

After they left, I slowly walked over to Porchia's bed, and her face hardened. She just stared at me as I poured out my heart to her. In return, she asked for me to give her some time. She basically dismissed me and told me she would call me when she was ready to talk.

I did not blame her for her reaction, because I knew that I deserved it. But I was hell-bent on doing everything possible to make it up to her. I told her I would give her as much time as she needed. I walked out the room with my head hanging down. Aunt Hattie looked at me and said, "Boy, you look like you lost your best friend. Baby Girl is up now. You should be happy."

I faked that I was happy and told them I would give them time to spend with Porchia. I told them that Porchia needed them more than she needed me at this time. They both hugged me and thanked me for being there.

As I was walking down the hall, the doctor approached me and asked me if he could speak with me. He informed me that he thought that Porchia would heal fine physically, but there may be some psychological damage due to the fact that she'd lost the baby during the accident. I must have looked at the doctor confused because he repeated what he said. He must have realized that I did not know, and he said, "I am so sorry for your loss. I thought you knew."

I had not only lost Porchia, but our baby as well. I sat in my car in the hospital parking lot and cried for hours. There could be no punishment that would be just for the pain I had caused. I'd killed an innocent child, my child! I started beating on the steering wheel until I got a call. It was Poo Man. He said, "Cuz, I have been trying to get in touch with Porchia for days. She has not returned my call. Do you know what's up?"

I responded, "I almost killed Porchia, and I killed our baby."

Poo Man asked me what I was talking about, and I told him I could not talk and hung up the phone. I went home and went to my bedroom and grabbed the sheets that Raheem and I had had sex on and threw them away. I then went to the guest room to contemplate my next move. I decided that I would get new bedroom furniture for my room because I would not be able to look at the bed anymore. Somewhere between my thoughts and drinking, I dozed off.

I woke up the next morning with two bottles of tequila next to me on the bed. I immediately called the hospital to find out about Porchia's condition, and the nurse told me she was recovering well. Her MRI showed that she was doing okay and the swelling around her brain had decreased significantly. I breathed a sigh of relief, knowing that Porchia was truly on the road to physical recovery. I just hoped that her heart would also heal soon and that she would find room to forgive me.

I heard some fumbling downstairs and got my gun because it sounded as if someone was breaking in. It was Poo Man, and he said, "What the hell is going on? You look like shit!"

I told him the story about Porchia getting hit by a truck and losing our baby.

"What? She was carrying yo' shorty?" asked Poo Man.

"Yeah. I didn't know anything about it."

"What happened?"

"I don't know Poo Man. But it has been a nightmare."

"Mane, I am here. What can I do? I want to go see her."

I told Poo Man where she was, and he ran out of the room shouting, "I'll be back soon!"

I sat around for hours, just thinking about what had transpired over the last week. I kept reliving the look on Porchia's face when she caught me with Raheem and how I found her lying lifeless in the street. Then I saw images of a little baby girl that looked just like Porchia. I saw visions of Poo Man being upset and disgusted by what happened. I knew that he would never forgive me for what I had done. I began feeling like I had caused a lot of pain for everyone. And although Porchia woke up, I knew that her life would be forever changed.

The idea just came to me. I put my plan into action by first calling the hospital to inquire about Porchia's bill. They gave me the amount, so I called the bank and asked them to send a bank draft to the hospital for more than the amount that was stated. It seemed like Porchia might have a few more days in the hospital, so I wanted to make certain she had no financial worries about the bill.

I found some paper and a pen and scribbled down: "Everyone will be better off without me. Pocahontas, I am so sorry for all the pain I have caused you. Know that I love you more than anything. Poo Man, thank you for being here for me. You have been not only a cousin and a brother, but a true friend. I am a tortured soul, and I choose not to torture anyone else."

After writing my note and putting it on the kitchen table, I went to the garage in search of something I could use. I found some twine that looked like it might work. I looked at the garage door motor and thought it would be strong enough to do the job. I found a chair that I could stand on. My plan was to kick it away so I could end it all. I tied the rope in a noose and put it around my neck to make certain it would work right. I then tied the rope to the steel portion of the garage door rail. I pulled it with all my strength to test whether it could hold my weight. It was sturdy. After everything was prepared and ready, I put my head in the noose, and just as I kicked the chair, my last thoughts were of Porchia and our baby.

****

I woke up to coughing and Poo Man leaning over me, shouting, "Mane, what the fuck were you trying to do!"

I guess I'd underestimated my weight. I had pulled down the railing of the garage door. I saw that a portion of the ceiling in the garage had collapsed. I started crying. I didn't know if it was because I had actually decided to end my life or because I had unsuccessfully attempted to do so. Poo Man struggled getting me up and into the kitchen to sit at the table. He poured me a glass of Hennessy and said, "Mane, you gotta get your shit together. You got everything to live for!"

At that moment, I could not even look at him. I put my face in my hands and just started crying. He came and hugged me and told me that he loved me and everything would be okay. He then called Aunt Verdie and said, "Mama, we need you." He took me upstairs, and I started protesting, saying I did not want to go into my room. So he took me to one of the guest rooms and put me on the bed. He handed me some pills and water and said, "Here take this."

I don't know what I took, but when I woke up, Aunt Verdie was sitting on the bed looking at me sternly. She said, "I will personally send you to meet your mother if you ever try something like that again."

I smiled and said, "Aunt Verdie, nice to see you too. I am sorry. Life just got in my way for a minute."

She looked at me and said, "Boy, when it gets too hard to stand, do like your mom used to do … just kneel."

I had to pull myself together because we were having a home game that evening. I called the hospital and found out that Porchia was being released. Poo Man and Aunt Verdie decided that they would stay with me for the week. It was exciting to have them at my game, but my mind was on Porchia during the entire game.

In my preoccupation, I scored thirty-two points, had twelve assists, got thirteen boards, and five blocks. Aunt Verdie and Poo Man screamed the entire game.

The guys teased me after the game, saying that I should have them at every game, because evidently family boosted my performance. I didn't know what happened, but I had turned into an animal on the court.

After the game, I called the hospital, and they confirmed that Porchia had been released. I called Mystery and found out that they were already back in Houston. I asked her to give Porchia my love and to tell her I would get to Houston as soon as my schedule allowed.

I arrived three days later to see Porchia, only to have her turn me away and tell me that I should wait for her to contact me before I came to Houston again. I wrote her several letters, called her several times, sent several e-mails, and sent flowers, but I never received a response. In my heart, I knew that Porchia would never forgive me. But I also knew that I would never stop trying to seek forgiveness, even if we would never be together in the manner I desired.

Chapter 17

Aunt Verdie pleaded with me to seek professional help to get me through the rough times I was experiencing. Although I was pretending to be happy, she saw right through the tortured soul living inside of me. No one knew why Porchia was hit by that truck, except Raheem. I couldn't share the truth with anyone. After the incident, I completely distanced myself from Raheem. He served as a constant reminder of everything I'd lost. The bottom line was, Raheem was just a self-centered, egotistical, narcissistic maniac who cared about no one but himself. After the incident with Porchia, he called me several times, telling me to make certain Porchia said nothing to anyone about what she'd seen. I told him to never speak to me again, unless it was something related to our roles as teammates.

I acted upon Aunt Verdie's advice and sought professional counseling. It took some searching, but I was able to find a black male psychiatrist who had been molested by an older male, who also happened to be gay. If I did not know any of these facts, there was no evidence that Dr. Mouton had ever been molested or that he was gay. He seemed to be your typical black married professional heterosexual male with 2.5 kids who had a home in the suburbs and was living the dream. In fact, Dr. Mouton lived in the suburbs with his male lover of twenty years, had no kids, enjoyed all sports, and was an avid golfer. One thing that I admired about Dr. Mouton was his confidence in who he was.

It took a little while for me to open up to him, but once I did, I found out that he really could relate to my situation. I think more than anything, during our sessions, I realized that I also had a choice about my life and the way I chose to live it. I did not have to live up to anyone else's expectations, but the expectations I'd set for myself. I decided to set standards for myself. I decided that I would live according to God's word. Dr. Mouton also introduced me to his church in Birmingham.

His pastor, Dr. James High, was young and progressive. He accepted and loved everyone as they were, but he also spoke the truth. He spoke adamantly against homosexuality, bisexuality, adultery, fornication, and all of the evils and sins that the Bible talked about. Although he knew that his large congregation included gays and lesbians, he did not mince his words and often proclaimed that the wages for sin was death. Everything he taught was Bible-based. He challenged his congregation to become familiar with the way that God desired for everyone to live. He encouraged his congregation to seek their own understanding of what he presented to us. He reinforced the principle that understanding the Bible was the key to developing a healthy relationship with God. One of his favorite scriptures was Proverbs 3:5-6: "Trust in the Lord with all your heart, and lean not on your own understanding; In all your ways acknowledge Him, and He shall direct your paths." I frequently recited this passage to help myself through the challenges I faced.

Dr. Mouton's and my sessions were not limited to talking about me; we also had philosophical discussions about world issues. The one thing that I discovered about myself was that I was attempting to be what others expected me to be, and during my sessions, I found out who I was. I was a man who was abused by another man, but this did not define my sexuality. My sexuality was a choice that I could make. My circumstances did not dictate who and what I was or who and what I was to become.

I enjoyed having sex with men, but the most enjoyable sex I had was with the woman that I loved. I remember each time after having sex with men, it was over. There was nothing left after the sex but memories of pleasure. With Porchia, we made love without ever even touching. I understood that I wanted this type of relationship, preferably with Porchia. I had never met anyone that made me feel the way that she did. If I could not have a relationship with Porchia again, I would not have a relationship with another person until I felt those same feelings.

115

I decided that I would reach out to Porchia and share my whole story with her. She would either accept me or reject me. That was the risk I was willing to take to pursue happiness in a relationship with her. I was surprised when Porchia agreed to meet with me. I told her all about Rico and every other lover I'd had in my life. I spilled out all of the feelings I had for her. To my surprise, she was understanding, but not willing to accept that I would never fall for another man. What Porchia failed to understand was that I probably would never ever fall for another person. I left feeling like I had probably lost her forever, but at least, she knew where I stood.

****

Some time elapsed, and I had not spoken to Porchia. Raheem called me all panicked about his wife and Porchia meeting at Georgetown and sharing a room together for a week. I knew nothing about what Porchia was doing. I had been concentrating on the playoffs and getting myself whole again.

Raheem shared with me that Porchia had decided to go to Georgetown on a full academic scholarship. I told Raheem that he did not have to worry about Porchia because she was a very classy lady, who was probably the complete opposite of any woman that he knew. I reminded him that we were not to talk outside the court about anything other than things that affected the team. He ended the conversation with, "I won't go down by myself. Just remember that son!"

After the conversation with Raheem, I decided to reach out to Porchia one more time. I left her a message telling her that I had grown significantly since I had been in counseling. I also told her that I loved her, but more than anything, I needed for her to forgive me for what I had done to her. I never heard back from her, so I decided that I would leave it in God's hand, knowing that He would direct my next steps.

Shortly after that, Poo Man called me to tell me that Aunt Hattie had passed. I asked Poo Man to make certain that Porchia was okay and to pass on the funeral arrangements to me. By any means necessary, I knew I had to be there for Porchia. She probably felt that she was all alone in the world. Although Mystery was her mother, I knew that Porchia had not bonded with her as a daughter should have. I wanted Porchia to know that, even if we were not together, I would be there in her time of need.

When I saw Porchia, I had more anxiety than I had when I went out on the floor for my first NBA game. I sat in the car and watched her go into the church. I did not want to go in the church and cause a disturbance, so I just sat in the car until I found the right time to give Porchia my condolences. Poo Man and I rode out to the cemetery together. Porchia, even through her sadness, looked more beautiful than I remembered.

After the short ceremony at the cemetery, Porchia was left alone. I saw the perfect opportunity to speak with her. I sent Poo Man as an intermediary to get her to the car. Once she came to the car and saw me, her face hardened. I begged her to let us drive her to the repast. She finally agreed, but she made Poo Man sit between the two of us. I kept looking at her using my peripheral vision. My mind may have been playing tricks on me, but it seemed like she was also looking at me from the corner of her eyes.

Once we arrived at the repast site, Porchia told Poo Man that she needed to speak with me alone. I was shocked to hear those words coming out of her mouth, but I could not have been happier. I hoped that this would be our road to recovery. She asked me to take her to a place where we could have a private conversation. I decided to take her to one of my favorite restaurants where I knew I would be guaranteed a private area. We ordered wine and talked like old times.

I was feeling good about where we were headed until Porchia said, "Ty, I am in a very different space. I need to find out who I am and what I want. You were my first and only love. But I am still young and not ready to commit to anyone. Well, I have committed to someone … God. He is the only man in my life right now. I am listening to Him and following His lead."

I could not contest anything she said because I was in the very same space. I was listening to God and following His lead, as well. I just hoped that He would lead Porchia my way. I told her I wanted to be there as her friend until she figured out I was the only one for her. She laughed, and we both left the restaurant in a good space. I was not quite certain that Porchia would ever open up the door for us again, but in that moment, I believed that we both would be all right.

Chapter 18

I returned to Birmingham with the Rookie of the Year title, but I was not quite certain I was ready for the playoffs. I was a little anxious about what faced me. I was accustomed to the lights and glory, but not mentally prepared for this next step. Unfortunately, my team had to travel because we had the worst record of all of the playoff teams in our division. That did not bother me as much as it bothered others on the team because I was glad that, as an expansion team, we were contenders.

However, I was exhausted from fighting off the groupies, understanding my feelings about Porchia, and trying to figure out what I needed to do to be a motivator to help the team to succeed at the next level. I called Dr. Mouton to see if I could get an appointment before I left for our road trip. Dr. Mouton's assistant set up an appointment for me for the next day.

When I arrived at his office, his assistant told me she had called me to reschedule because Dr. Mouton had to attend to an emergency. I must have looked deflated because she hurriedly said, "If you need to speak someone today, Dr. Merlino is here and can see you."

"No, I would not feel comfortable speaking to anyone but Dr. Mouton."

Just as I completed my sentence, a woman walked out and said, "Don't knock it 'til you try it."

I looked up and saw a mocha-complexioned, six foot, shapely woman with long, flowing black hair, and high cheekbones with dimples. She was wearing red stilettos with a red and white pantsuit that complimented her curves. I must have stared at her for about five minutes without saying a word.

She extended her hand out to me and said, "Hello. I am Dr. Merlino."

I stuttered, "Hel-l-lo. I am Ty-ty-rese."

I know I must have sounded like a blabbering idiot. She said, laughing, "I should be the one stuttering." She looked at her extended arm as if it would collapse if I did not shake her hand and said, "Well, Tyrese, it is a pleasure to meet you. If you would like to talk, as Stacy said, I am available."

I had never been caught so off guard by a female before. But her beauty was alarming. I finally shook her hand and said, "It's nice to meet you. But I really prefer to speak with Dr. Mouton." Then I ran out of the office like a little "biatch," like Poo Man would have said.

After I reached my car, I wondered, *What the hell was that all about?* I drove thinking about Dr. Merlino and my crazy reaction to her. I went home and found my housekeeper packing my clothes for the road. I called my barber to hook me up before I left. As I took care of some other errands, my mind was on Dr. Merlino the entire time.

I called Dr. Mouton's office and asked Stacy if Dr. Merlino was still available. She told me that she was not in the office, but she could take a message if I liked. I told her that was okay, I would call back. She said, "Okay, Mr. Gamble. Good luck with your game in Oklahoma."

I was so shocked that I didn't respond. I had not mentioned my name to her.

****

Later that evening, my phone rang, and the voice said, "Hello Mr. Gamble. I understand you called for me earlier."

I immediately recognized the voice and cussed Stacy out in my mind.

I gained my composure and said, "Well, hello, Dr. Merlino. I wanted to see if we could meet to speak about an opportunity."

"And what type of opportunity is that?" she asked.

"Well, I am starting a non-profit designed to help abused kids. I just thought someone with your qualifications could lend us a hand."

"Huh, I didn't think you knew anything about my qualifications since you ran out of the office earlier like I was a leper. But I must admit, I was hoping you were calling to ask me out to dinner," she said flirtatiously.

"I would love to discuss this opportunity over dinner if you would agree."

"Well, sure. Let me know when you are ready."

"I will. Thanks for calling me back."

"You are welcome, Mr. Gamble."

"Oh, please call me Ty."

"Only if you agree to call me promptly when you get back."

"I will do that Dr. Merlino," I said.

"Oh Ty," she said.

"Yes," I quickly answered.

"I am Jill to you."

"Okay. Well Jill, I look forward to seeing you again soon."

"Likewise."

After hanging up the phone, I was not certain who was coming on to whom. She seemed to be very direct. Realistically, I did not know if I was ready to pursue anyone new. After all, I was still trying to work through my feelings for Porchia. And I was still working on myself, getting to know who I was and what I wanted. I told myself that I refused to hurt another person the way I'd hurt Porchia, the one I'd professed to love and proclaimed to be ready to love for the rest of my life.

When I left for Oklahoma, I felt good about what was going on. I was not where I wanted to be, but I had faith that I would get there. I remembered, at one of the Dr. James High's Bible studies that I'd attended, he taught from Philippians 4:13, which basically stated that "I can do all things through Christ who strengthens me." When times got hard, I went back to this scripture and recited it repeatedly. Not only did I recite it, I believed it.

Although we lost the first two games in Oklahoma, the team came back confident that we could win the next two in Birmingham. We split the games at home and went back to Oklahoma and won one. We were excited about winning this game because, if we'd lost, our playoff hopes would have been lost. To our detriment, during the fourth quarter, our center went up for a rebound and came down and injured his ankle. As if that was not enough, Raheem cussed out one referee, shoved another one, and, as a result, was ejected for the remainder of the playoff series. We took the series back to Birmingham and lost. Overall, management was proud of our effort, and they figured that we could have won if we had not lost our center and shooting guard.

Although I was looking forward to advancing to the next round, with everything that I had experienced, I was now looking forward to some much-needed rest and relaxation. I also wanted to work with Coc on establishing my non-profit for abused children. I wanted, more than anything, to work on the reason I had decided to leave college in the first place. It would also give me a reason to get to know Jill better. I looked at my phone and realized that I'd missed a called from Mystery and Raheem.

Raheem left a message saying that I needed to call him as soon as possible because it was a matter of life or death. I figured he was just being his usual drama queenish self. But when I called him back, he told me he had AIDS and that he was going to reveal my name to the media as one of his partners. He said he was not going to be the only one that went down with this disease. I just hung up the phone. I knew that we had had protected sex. But I also knew that I would have to go get tested as soon as possible. I wondered how in the hell I'd ever allowed myself to get involved with such a narcissistic person.

I went to get tested early the following morning. While at lunch, I received a phone call telling me that my test was negative. I was relieved, but thought about what Raheem said he was going to do. I decided to just put it in God's hands and not worry about it.

Chapter 19

I was relaxing by my pool when the phone rang; it was Mystery. I forgot that she had called, and I had failed to return her phone call.

When I answered, she asked, "Is this Ty?"

My heart skipped a beat, thinking something may have happened to Porchia. I responded, "Hi, Mystery. Is everything okay?"

"Oh hey Ty. Everything is good. I am calling to invite you to Porchia's surprise eighteenth birthday party."

"Does she know that you are inviting me?"

"No, silly. It's a surprise, so I am not saying anything."

"I am sure this surprise will be priceless. What day and time?"

I assured Mystery that I would be there and thought to myself that this would be the perfect time to make certain that Porchia and I were done, before moving on.

****

When I arrived in Houston, I was impressed by the venue. Mystery and Sweezy, Chanti's boyfriend before she died, had an extravagant place in Houston. Mystery excitedly showed me around the club and introduced me to people who I had no interest in meeting. But I had never seen her so happy, and she had never been more pleasant to be around. I recalled the days when she thought I was a two-bit hustler and had treated me as such. I'd never understood why she was so protective of Porchia until now.

There was a crowd of about eighty people, all waiting for Porchia's arrival. When she arrived, we all shouted, "Surprise!"

I knew by the look on her face that she did not appreciate the surprise, but she was gracious and pretended to be happy in everyone's presence. She looked so sexy in the dress that I had purchased for her that I had never seen her wear. When she finally got the chance to greet me, she seemed genuinely happy to see me.

I got caught up in talking to some of Porchia's teammates who adored her. But what caught my attention was Porchia speaking to some guy who seemed to be a little too interested in her. I watched her body language to see if she was as interested in him as he was with her; but I could not tell because Porchia always played it so cool. When she approached me, I wanted to ask her who exactly this guy was but thought she would probably would cuss me out for having the audacity to ask her that question. We were getting along so well, and I didn't want to take the chance of messing up the lovely time I was spending with her.

Porchia looked as if she had seen a ghost after Mystery announced that she was engaged to Sweezy. I immediately went to Porchia to take her away from the situation before she blew up. She asked me to take her home, and we talked on the way there. I tried to calm her down, but she insisted that Mystery did not care who she hurt or how she hurt them. I knew that Mystery would not intentionally try to hurt Porchia, but Porchia had made up her mind about Mystery's intentions. I was hoping that this occurrence would allow me to spend some time with Porchia alone at Aunt Hattie's, but she made it clear to me that she preferred to be alone.

I knew that I had gotten my answer from Porchia. She still was not ready to give us another chance. I left Houston sad; but confident that, if I moved on, Porchia would not care. Despite it all, I knew, in my heart, that I would always love Porchia. In the words of the illustrious Dolly Parton's song (which reached a new generation of people through the late great songstress, Whitney Houston) "I Will Always Love You" was in my head for weeks after leaving her.

When I returned to Birmingham, I set up an appointment with Dr. Mouton. I was having very mixed feelings about what happened in Houston. I wanted to stay and beg Porchia to give us another chance, but I had done this numerous times and had only received the same rejection. At the same time, I wanted to move on, but not quite certain how to make that happen when all I thought about was Porchia. Yes,

Jill had caught my eye, but whose eyes would she not catch. My session with Dr. Mouton made me realized that I needed to take care of me first. I would not be any good to any other person without completely healing and being good to myself. I decided that I would not call Jill, but would keep focusing on myself.

I also decided that I wanted to make certain that I started my nonprofit for abused kids. I contacted a few of the organizations I knew that specialized in healthy living for abused kids to get advice about what was needed. I buried myself in making certain that my dream of a successful organization for children evolved as I had planned prior to entering the NBA. I hit up Dr. Mouton for a person he would recommend to lead my effort. He referred me to a friend in Atlanta that he thought would be a perfect fit for the position.

Terry, my driver, drove me to Atlanta to meet with the potential new director of my nonprofit Rising Above. RJ Bartholomew definitely had my vote to lead the charge. Bart, as he liked to be called, came from a family with money, but, as a child, had been abused by his mother. He did not go into specifics, but the way that Bart spoke about Mommy Bartholomew made Tio Rico seem like Mother Teresa.

He was a young, rude white boy with an edge that would have frightened the average suburban person. However, Bart had brilliant ideas, the skills and experience to make sure he carried out Rising Above's mission. He also assured me that he would keep me involved as much as I wanted to be. This was one of my life's dreams, and I definitely not only wanted to be involved, but wanted to personally ensure that the organization would be successful.

Bart and I went to the club, Game Changer, later on that evening to celebrate our newly formed relationship. Game Changer was owned by an ex-Falcon football player and was one of Atlanta's hottest clubs, the place where everybody was somebody. I met a couple of record executives, players who I played with, some current Falcons, bankers, and a few Fortune 500 executives. I must have caught the attention of one of the executives from one of the largest beverage companies in America. I was full on that brown liquor and probably responded to his advances, because when I went to the bathroom, the brother followed me there. He offered me some powder, and I told him I did not do that shit. He came up close and said, "I bet you wanna do this shit," and grabbed his crouch.

I pushed him back and said, "Man, I definitely ain't into that shit."

He pushed back on me and said, "Man, I can make your eyes roll to the back of your head."

Before I knew it, I was beating him down until he was bloody and not moving. Bart came into the bathroom, screaming, "Bro, what the fuck are you doing?"

I yelled, "This punk azz muthafuka just tried to come on to me."

"Bro, you want an assault charge on your azz? This shit is whack man!"

"I bet yo' faggot azz won't try that shit on nobody no mo'," I screamed while kicking him in his groan area.

"Come on, bro. We need to bounce. I will get someone to take care of him."

Bart led me out of the club and to my car. He looked at me and said, "Bro, I don't know what that was all about. But you gotta keep it together. You are in the public eye."

I thanked him and told him that I would be in touch soon. I told Terry to drive me back to Birmingham, although we were supposed to stay in Atlanta for one more day. Terry had a lot of questions about what happened, but I told him I did not feel like talking about it. I needed to get back to my own familiarity, and I needed to have an emergency counseling session with Dr. Mouton. I was not certain what happened at that club because violence was not part of my DNA. Afterward, I felt bad for attacking that poor man. I somewhat felt that he was only reacting to vibes he felt from my sexual energy.

Chapter 20

Porchia surprised me with a call, telling me that she had decided to go to seminary school. This was an about-face from the girl I knew that would cuss out a fly if it got in her way. She told me the story of meeting God when she got into the accident. She said she was led to go a very different way after meeting what she referred to as "The Light." It made me feel good that Porchia called me to tell me about her very important life decision. Although I was shocked at her life-changing decision, I told her I supported her in whatever she decided to do.

Months after my conversation with Porchia, I ran into her and Mystery at a hotel in Charlotte. All of the feelings came rushing back when I laid my eyes on her. I had begun casually dating, but I was not serious about anyone. It was a pleasant surprise to see Porchia and Mystery getting along. I observed them, and they acted as if they were best friends. Mystery had an amazing glow about herself and looked happier than I had ever seen her. I asked both of them to join me for dinner. Mystery quickly accepted, while Porchia grudgingly agreed.

We had such a good time at dinner that I did not want my visit with them to end. So I asked them both out to a club that I had heard about. Porchia and I danced and talked like we had not done in a long time. She asked about whether Raheem had calmed down on his threats to reveal that I was his lover. I told her that was long behind me and that Raheem was being traded from the team.

I did not want to leave without knowing whether Porchia and I could rekindle our relationship, so I thought I would make my feelings known.

"Pocahontas, life has not been the same without you."

"My life is not the same without you," responded Porchia.

"Why can't we work it out?" I asked.

"Ty, I am trying to work it out with God right now."

"You don't have time for me and God? It sure looked like you had time for that guy at your party."

"Ty, when I am with you, you take over my life. I would not have time for anything or anybody else. I still love you Ty. But I am choosing to follow where God leads me right now."

Once Porchia laid it down like that, I felt I could do nothing but respect her wishes.

Before we parted, we had the most passionate kiss that I had ever experienced. I wished it would have led to more, but Porchia made it clear — this was as far as it was going to go with us. She left me with the words, "Perhaps in a different time, in a different place." I felt a tear rolling down my face as she left me standing in the elevator.

I was in Charlotte because I was a groomsman in a wedding. The groom was one of my home boys who played for the Panthers. At the reception the next day, I was feeling a little down about me and Porchia's interaction. One of my partna's teammates asked me what was up with me. I wrote it off as feeling under the weather. He told me I looked like Lady Day when she was locked up in prison in Lady Sings the Blues.

For once in my life, I did not feel like faking it. I looked at him and told him that was exactly how I felt. I was in no mood for a wedding reception. I was about to leave when I heard, "The night is still early. Where are you going, Your Majesty?" I looked up, and there she was with a big smile on her face.

"Hey, Lese! What are you doing here?" I walked up to her and gave her a big hug.

"Keeping an eye on you," Lisa said.

"How did you know I needed keeping?"

"I feel you, Mr. Gamble. I feel you when you think I ain't even looking."

"Girl, I see you have not changed. You may be just what the doctor ordered. So what have you been up to?"

"Well, if you can take me out for a drink, I will tell you all about it. Then may serve you a little medicine too."

I laughed and reached out my arm to her and said, "It would be my pleasure for you to take me away from here."

Lisa found her ride to tell her that she would be leaving. Lisa and I decided to go back to her hotel for a drink. There was a jazz quartet playing some smooth jams. It created the perfect atmosphere for talking and relaxing. I found out that Lisa was writing under an assumed name for the newspaper *Politico*. She often stirred up a lot of controversy in the District, and thought she could express herself more freely if her name was not revealed.

She was living the life of a bachelorette in Chocolate City. According to Lisa, D.C. had gone from Chocolate City to Swinger City. She shared some of the funny, failed sexcapades she had experienced while living there. We talked until the club closed. Lisa looked at me and told me that she was not ready for the night to end. I honestly was not ready for the night to end either. So when she asked if we could take the party to her room, I happily complied; despite my mind screaming no. In that moment, I swore I heard R Kelly say, "I don't see nothing wrong, with a little bump and grind."

Lisa got what she wanted, me naked in her bed, and her taking advantage of me. However, I found myself enjoying the sexual experience, too. The girl was a sex machine. She kept me going for hours. We did it doggy and froggy style, from the front, back, and anally. Just when I thought we were done, she would do something to arouse me again.

I was glad that another woman, besides Porchia, could get a rise from me. And it must have also been good to her 'cause she sang my name from night 'til the morning. I knew the entire floor would be singing a new song called "Ty." In fact, it was much better than I could have ever imagined, and it definitely ran rings around what happened when we were drunk in college.

Before creeping out of her room the next morning, Lisa and I exchanged numbers and promised that we would stay in contact. I had to question God's motive in letting me run into two of my exes in the same city. Lisa was a very vivacious, exciting lady, but still, she was not Porchia.

I knew there would come a time when I would have to stop comparing every lady I met to Porchia, but right now was not that time. With Porchia, everything was natural. It was not difficult to talk with her or make love to her. Until I found something as natural as what I shared with Porchia, I knew I would not get seriously involved with anyone.

On my way back to Birmingham, I thought about how lonely my existence would be without someone to share it with. The little devil on my shoulder told me I was rich, young, and famous, and that I could have any woman, or for that matter, man, I desired. The fact was, I only wanted one woman. And in my heart, I felt that one day I would get her.

Just as I was dreaming about Porchia, the flight attendant passed me a note with his number on it. I wondered what made men think it was okay to flirt with me. I'd just gotten through banging a freak for six hours, so how was "gay" written on my forehead? I could not let my emotions get the best of me this time, but I wanted to beat this dude down!

He passed back by with a smug look on his face. I looked directly in his face and tore the note into pieces with an I-WILL-FUCK-YOU-UP look. He turned up his nose, lifted his head, and twisted away. I realized I really needed to discuss my reaction with Dr. Mouton. Was I putting out something toward gay men that made them react this way? I thought I presented myself as a card-carrying heterosexual alpha-male. Perhaps, not having a woman by my side was the trigger for them to come on to me. Whatever it was, I wanted it to stop!

Chapter 21

I successfully avoided Jill for weeks, but one day as I was walking out of Dr. Mouton's office, I ran into her in the hallway. She looked me up and down and said, "Hey, stranger, if I did not know better, I would think you were trying to renege on our dinner date."

"No, I have just been busy. You are looking good, as usual. How have you been?" I asked.

"Lonely, waiting on your call."

She caught me off guard with that response. I nervously laughed and said, "A beautiful woman like you should never be lonely. We could rectify this situation by setting up a date now."

"Well, I need to check my calendar."

"Oh, you sweating a brother, but now you gotta check your calendar?"

"You know I gotta play hard to get after you put me on ice all this time."

"Okay. Okay. So how about tomorrow for dinner?" I asked.

"Okay, so call me with the details."

"I will call you later on this evening, doctor."

"It's Miss Doctor to you, if you nastay," she laughed. "I will be waiting for your call," she winked and strutted away.

I thought to myself, *Wow, this lady is gonna be a handful.*

I called Jill later that evening and made arrangements to pick her up for dinner at seven the following evening. I did not want her to think I was pretentious, so I decided to drive us to dinner, instead of using Terry. The fact of the matter was that I did not like driving, so that was why I'd hired Terry, who was a friend from high school who was down on his luck.

I had been hiring drivers from companies, but when Terry came to visit me, we talked and made a mutually beneficial agreement for him to be my driver. He doubled as an assistant, as well. I paid him a good salary, and now he lived independently and supported his four children and three baby mamas back in Beaumont. In addition, I trusted Terry with things I would not trust others with. However, I did not trust the intimate details of my life with anyone but Dr. Mouton. It made me wonder if dating Jill would compromise our doctor-patient relationship.

When I arrived at Jill's house, she was wearing a form-fitting black mini dress with gold stilettos and matching gold accessories. It amazed me how comfortable she felt wearing high heels with her height. Most tall women I knew tried to downplay their height, but she accented it, which made her stand out even more. And it was, as my Oaktown teammate always said, "hella" attractive to me. What first attracted me to Porchia was her personality, whereas Jill's beauty was simply captivating. When she opened the door, I said, "So I guess you are ready to go Golden Beauty."

She smiled and said, "If you prefer, we could just take off our clothes and stay here."

I think she enjoyed watching me squirm and stutter. I quickly recovered from my stupor and replied, "And not let the world be jealous of me? No way. We are going out so every man can envy me."

She laughed and said, "Oh, you are good Tyrese Gamble."

We walked to the car, and I opened the door for her. After closing her door, I thought, *Ooh, this night is gonna be a long one.*

Keeping with the theme of the night, non-pretentiousness, I chose one of my favorite restaurants, Satterfield's. The food was excellent, and the staff was even better. I knew they would accommodate me in a private area of the restaurant where we could enjoy our dinner without fan interruption. It turned out that this was one of Jill's favorites, as well. She surprised me by being on first name basis with most of the staff.

I found Jill, not only to be amazingly beautiful, but intelligent as well. Her mother was from Trinidad, and her father was a second-generation Italian from Philadelphia. She told the story about how her father had visited Trinidad and fallen in love with her mother at first sight. Her mother was only sixteen, and her dad was twenty-six years old. Her dad spent five years trying to get her over to the United States, so he could marry her.

Jill's parents had been married for thirty-four years until her father mysteriously appeared floating in the Schuylkill River. As a child, she never understood what her father did for a living, but as an adult, she found out that he was a boss for one of the major Italian mafia groups within Philadelphia. Her entire life had been unknowingly financed by the "family."

I listened to her stories and knew that our lives were as far apart as two people's lives could be. She went to the best schools, had a nanny, took vacations to Europe to connect with her family in Italy, and even spent two years traveling abroad after graduating from college. The most astonishing part of the night was finding out that Jill was ten years my senior.

I assumed that she may have been six years older than me since she had completed medical school and was a practicing psychiatrist, but she looked phenomenal for her age. I asked Jill had she ever been married, and she told me that she had been engaged twice. According to Jill, she stood up one guy at the altar after finding out he was sleeping with her best friend. The other guy was already married, and he had a wife and kids that lived in Ghana. Jill said that she had stopped dating about two years ago because she realized that she was attracting the same type of guys over and over again. She sought counseling and came to the conclusion that she needed to work on herself to be able to recognize a good man for herself. She told me that I was the first guy that she had ever gone out on a date with since she'd made her decision to not date and be celibate with the hope of coming in touch with her inner being. She laughed and said, "I guess I sort of forced you into this date because, obviously, you were not interested."

Because Jill seemed so honest and sincere, I also confided in her and told her that I was working on myself, too, and did not want to have a beautiful woman like her to distract me from reaching my goal of knowing who I was or what I wanted. I poured out my heart to her about Porchia. I felt so comfortable with Jill that I also told her about my sexual escapades with men. She did not judge me or seem surprised. Instead, she told me that life was a series of battles; some of them were internal, while others were external. Jill was very skilled at what she did, she took out the heaviness in the air by saying, "We will only win the war if we are able to look in the mirror and be proud of what the mirror reflects back. And I bet you'd probably really like what you saw in the mirror, if you worked on your game outside of the perimeter."

"Oh, so now you are saying my outside game is weak!"

"Yeah, dude, you seem to limit your game to inside the post. I know you can do better than that."

"And you are an expert on my game, why?"

"Because I was instrumental in making certain that Birmingham got an expansion team, and y'all went to the first round and blew it. You were expected to lead us to the second round."

"Oh, dayuum! Sorry for disappointing you. I guess you will next tell me you are a part-owner of the team."

"If I were, you and I would have had this talk long before now," she laughed.

Chapter 22

When we reached her house, I opened her car door and walked her to her front door. I was hoping that she would invite me in because I had really enjoyed our date, and she seemed to have enjoyed it as well. However, she unlocked her door and said, "I look forward to hearing from you when you have figured out who you are and what you want."

This was the first woman who had rejected me since Porchia, and it did not feel good. But she was right, I needed to work on myself. Even though it did not go as far as I would have liked it to have gone that night, I felt really good about being honest with her. She seemed to be the type of woman that I would like to spend the rest of my life with, if there was no Porchia. But she was right, I had to be sure about if I wanted a relationship with a woman.

As I was driving home, I received a call from my attorney, Coc, telling me that my biological father had died of a heart attack. The family contacted him to find out who he was when they found a couple of uncashed checks from him. Coc told them that he was representing someone. He said that he could not discuss the situation, but he would contact his client. I told Coc that he could tell them who I was, but also tell them not to contact me.

I knew that, if they contacted me, they would only want to pimp me for money like my sperm donor did. I wrote in the sperm donor's contract that there was no contingency for anyone to receive money after his death. I drove home angry, thinking that Coc should have handled the situation without contacting me. I'd made my feelings known long ago; I wanted nothing to do with my sperm donor or his family.

When I got home, Terry called to see how my date went with Jill. I gave him a watered-down version of events and told him that we planned on seeing each other again. I called Aunt Verdie the next day to tell her that my attorney had called to let me know that my biological father had died. Aunt Verdie had already heard the news through the grapevine. She also said that she'd heard that they did not know anything about me until after his death. According to Aunt Verdie, they just thought that I was a player from the area that might have been a distant cousin. I realized that the greedy bastard did not share the news with anyone because he did not want to share his money.

Coc left me a message saying that I had two older brothers and one younger sister. The younger sister, who was eight years old, called him and said that she'd heard that she had another brother and wanted to meet him. I called him back and told him I did not have any interest in meeting any of them. Then, I called Aunt Verdie and told her what happened. She told me that I should sleep on it and not make any rash decisions. She also reminded me that my brothers and sisters did not have anything to do with what their father had done to my mother.

I had an appointment with Dr. Mouton, and he could tell that something was bothering me beyond the usual things that we discuss. I told him that my biological father had died and that the family had reached out to me and asked that I attend the funeral. This was the first time that I realized I'd never had a male role model in my life besides my coach in high school. My grandfather, uncles, and older male relatives never served in that role for me. And I had a lot of animosity toward my father, for not only abandoning my mother, but for abandoning me. I was punishing those who were not involved because I couldn't punish those who needed to be punished. These people were just as much a part of my bloodline as Poo Man, who I would die for.

I called Coc to get the number that my sister, Penny, had left for me to call. When I called her, she squealed so loud it hurt my ears. She told me that her brothers had been in and out of jail since she was born, and she always wanted a "real" big brother. She said that she was so excited when she found out that she, not only had another big brother, but a big brother who was famous. The girl must have talked for fifteen minutes before I could say one word. She begged me to attend the funeral for my sperm donor. I had a difficult time refusing her pleas, so I agreed to attend.

I received a surprise call from Jill telling me that she was attending a convention in Houston. At the end of our conversation, she said that she would like to accompany me to my dad's funeral. I started wondering about the confidentiality that Dr. Mouton and I shared, until Jill explained to me that she'd read about my father's death in a magazine called The Gossip.

She told me I was on the cover and the story inside said that my mother was a teenage whore who had seduced married men. I became highly upset and told her that I would sue them for libel. They did not know what they were talking about. It was the opposite — my father seduced a young teenage girl and left her pregnant.

Jill tried to comfort me by saying I was lucky that this was the first time I was a headliner in The Gossip, and that the story was not as scandalous as some other articles she'd read about other celebrities. She told me there was a story in the same edition about Raheem Shivers's wife divorcing him because she'd caught him in bed with the pool guy. The article also went on to say that Raheem was being released from his latest contract because he was nothing but a distraction to the NBA. I told her that I guess that not all of The Gossip stories are fabricated. She laughed and asked me to send her my airline reservations, so she could book her flight at the same time I was leaving.

When I called the airlines, I booked two first-class, one-way tickets to Houston. I did not know when I would be returning and did not have information on when Jill wanted to return. I e-mailed our itinerary to Jill, and she called me in return with a thank-you, but told me it was not necessary for me to pay for her ticket. I told Jill that I was happy that she wanted to go to the funeral with me. I was not looking forward to going alone, so paying for her ticket was just a simple act of gratitude toward her kind actions. I had planned on calling Poo Man and telling him I needed him to do me a favor. But having a beautiful woman on my arm would be just the distraction I needed to get through the ordeal of meeting my other family for the first time.

Terry wanted to go, so he could drive me around, but I wanted to avoid the celebrity-like appearance. I decided to rent an SUV at the Intercontinental Airport and drive to Port Arthur. Poo Man called me and told me that he would join me, but I told him I had a date. He asked whether it was Porchia, and I told him that Porchia had written me off. He reminded me that he had not wanted me to mess with Porchia in the first place. I told him I knew that, but I could not do anything but follow my heart. He told me that I had followed my dick, instead of my heart. I wished what he had said was true because it would have been much easier to let Porchia go.

The funeral was supposed to start at 11:00 a.m., so I decided to arrive thirty minutes late to avoid the awkwardness of meeting family for the first time at the church. When we arrived, the family was standing outside. A little chocolate girl with curly long locks, big light brown eyes, and round cheeks with dimples looked my direction, pointed, and said, "See! I told y'all that he would come." She ran to me, hugged me tightly around my legs, and said, "Hello, brother."

I looked at Jill, and she was smiling. I hugged the child back and said, "Hello, and you must Penny."

Penny grabbed my hand and led me to the other people standing outside and said, "I asked them to wait for you. I knew you would make it. Look everybody, Ty is here!"

I waved at the group of people, and they smiled and greeted me one by one. I thought I had seen a ghost when Penny's mother introduced herself to me. She was the spitting image of an older version of my mother. I know I must have stared at her a little too long because she broke the embarrassment by saying, "It is truly an honor to meet you. Penny has been talking about you since she found out that she had another brother."

I looked at her and said, "Thank you, ma'am. It is a pleasure to meet you, too. And this is my friend Jill."

Jill reached out her hand and shook Penny's mother's hand and said, "How do you do, ma'am?"

She reached out and said, "My name is Eurice, and it is nice to meet you, Jill."

I noticed a boy who looked like he was about twenty-six years old hanging back, wearing sagging pants, a white tee, and white Converse tennis shoes. I assumed that this was my brother, but he made no effort to come toward me.

Ms. Eurice looked at Penny and said, "Is it okay for us to go in now, Ms. Penny?"

"Yes, Mother. Now that Ty is here, we can go in."

She came and took my hand and Jill's hand and said, "Ty, can you and Ms. Jill sit by me?"

I looked at Ms. Eurice, and she smiled and nodded her head.

"Sure, Penny. We would love to sit by you."

Chapter 23

By the time I left Port Arthur, I had fallen in love with a third lady. Penny was the sweetest and most well-mannered child I had ever met. She kept saying "yes, sir" to me, and I asked her to just say "yes," and she said she could not do that to an older person. She wanted to know, instead, if she could say "yes, brother."

Her name for Jill became "My Jill," which Jill adored. It was as if Penny was born in another century; she was so loving and so innocent. Ms. Eurice was also a lovely lady. I wondered how such a despicable sperm donor could end up with two beautiful, loving women — my mother and Ms. Eurice.

The derelict was my brother, Tyrone, who barely said two words to me. I found out that my other brother, Tyrelle Jr., was currently serving thirty years to life in Angola Prison for raping a white girl. The family said she was really his rich, white under-aged girlfriend who lived in Jena, Louisiana. I thought, *Son, like father.* My mother was under-aged when she was impregnated by my sperm donor.

My sperm donor's parents were deceased, and I had only one uncle. My uncle, Thomas Gamble, was a Wall

Street investor who lived in NYC and did not have much contact with his brother. We exchanged numbers, and he said he wanted to make certain that I was investing in the right things because basketball would not last forever. He was definitely all business and left immediately after the funeral.

I spoke with Ms. Eurice about Uncle Tom, and she told me that he had married a white woman, but they were now divorced. She went on to say luckily they did not have any children. I did not know whether she said that because they were now divorced or because the woman was white. I knew the women in my family made it a big deal anytime anyone married someone of another race. This was one of the reason I usually dated either black or multi-racial women with African ancestry,

Jill acted as if she was the supportive woman in my life. She was very attentive to all of Penny's needs and made certain I was also taken care of. At the repast, she made my plate and got up several times to get me other things, such as drinks and desserts. I watched her work the room with her infectious smile and grace.

I think that most people were enamored with her, more so than they were excited about me being there; although I had a couple of folks ask for pictures and autographs. When the crowd started bothering me too much, Penny stood up, put her hands on her hips, and said, "Now, kind people, my brother needs a rest from all of this."

I smiled and thought to myself that she did a better job of protecting me than some of the body guards I'd hired in the past.

Before leaving, Tyrone came over and said, "It is good that you took some time out of your busy schedule to come to pop's funeral. He told me he tried to contact you, and you blew him off." He put his hand on his waistband and patted it and said, "I just wanna warn you, this better be you last time coming here."

I took a deep breath and said, "You gonna have to come betta than that. We all gotta go one day." I stepped closer to him and looked him dead in his eyes and said, "But I want you to know there are three sides to every story. If one day you would like to hear mine, hit me up."

Penny came over and begged me to stay for a little while longer. I told her I had other meetings to attend, but I would get back to visit her as soon as possible. I felt bad for lying to her, but there was no way I was going to stay a day longer. I found Ms. Eurice and thanked her for letting me spend time with the family. She told me that she was glad that I made it because I was all that Penny had been talking about.

Jill was busy talking to some women as if they were her best friends. I went over and said, "Darling, we need to go now. You will miss your appointment, if we don't leave now."

Jill looked at me and said, "Oh, dear, I almost forgot. Excuse me, ladies, but it was a pleasure speaking with you. Give me a call if you are ever in

Birmingham," and proceeded to give all of them her business card.

I looked back at Penny, and she had tears in her eyes. In spite of my brother's threat, I knew that I would have to come see her again. I went over, picked her up, and said, "I will come back soon if you give me a big smile."

She showed me all of her teeth and said, "I am going to miss you Brother. Please make it back soon."

"I will, Princess." From that day on, I began calling her Princess.

Jill reached over and kissed Penny on her forehead and said, "You take care of your mommy, okay?"

"I will My Jill. I love you."

"I love you too sweetie."

I wondered, *What is happening in my life? I have a little sister I adore and a lovely lady by my side that I admire.*

Jill talked about how much she enjoyed hanging out with me and my other family. I told her that she was a champ at entertaining. She spoke highly of Penny and said that she had always wanted a daughter just like her. I became curious as to where she stood at this point in her life.

So I asked, "So, Jill, are you ready to settle down?"

"Yes, I am ready to settle down and start a family," she answered.

I don't know where the next question came from, but I asked, "So would you consider settling down with me?"

"What?" she asked.

"I did not stutter this time, did I? Would you consider settling down with me?"

"Ty, we have not even dated! And you are supposed to be figuring out what you want."

"Well, it does not take me long to figure out what I want. Are you ambivalent?"

She remained silent for a while. Then, she said, "Yes, I would like to settle down with you. So what does settling down with you mean?"

"It means that I owe you a ring, a wedding date, and at least one baby."

"So, don't you find this a little odd?" she asked.

"Yeah, but it does not mean I don't want to do it," I said.

"Well, hell, planning has never worked for me. Let's just do it today."

"Today? Where can we get married today?" I asked.

"In Vegas. Let's fly to Vegas and get married."

"Are you shitting me?" I asked.

"No, I am dead serious," she said.

This time, I was silent. I always imagined that I would have dated the person for at least a year, gotten engaged in the second year, and married in the third year. By the time we married, we would know each other inside and out. We would be able to finish each other's sentences. We would know each other's favorite colors, favorite foods, who preferred the toilet roll under or over, which side of the bed we each preferred, and I knew none of this about Jill. I only knew that she was beautiful, charming, poised, spontaneous, assertive, honest, and intelligent. I admired her, but I did not love her. I did not even know what she was like in bed. How could I even think about marrying her, when the only person I ever dreamt of spending a lifetime with was Porchia?

"Okay, let's do it," I said.

The next thing I knew, we were headed back to the airport to catch a plane to Vegas. I asked Jill several times if she was sure she wanted to do this. She assured me that she could not be more certain that this was her destiny. She said, "Hell, I am more sure about this than I was about getting up this morning, flying with you to Texas, and having a great time at a funeral."

"Well, since you put it that way, can I have my first kiss, Ms. Soon-To-Be Mrs. Tyrese Gamble?"

"No, I want to save it for when we are pronounced husband and wife. And by the way, I am keeping my last name."

"You mean that you are hyphenating your last name?" I said.

"No, I mean that I am still going to be Jillian Gabriella Merlino."

I did not like the thought of that but decided that I would just handle that later.

Chapter 24

We arrived at the Palazzo Hotel in Vegas where I had already reserved the Lago Media suite. It was my favorite because it had a media room with a big screen TV. Jill was very happy with my choice and told me she could not wait to show her appreciation after the wedding. I arranged for a private wedding ceremony at the hotel to a woman whose full name I'd just learned, and who told me that she did not want my last name. I guess I would just have to learn everything else as time progressed.

I ran around trying to find the perfect ring set for our exchange of vows. As I entered the jewelry store, my phone rang. I answered it, and to my surprise, it was Porchia.

"Hey, there! What are you up to?"

"Um..."

"Wow! So what is um?" she asked.

"I am in Vegas."

"Oh, so are you getting married there, too?"

"What do you mean 'too'?"

"It was meant to be a joke. But Mystery and Sweezy were married there."

"Oh, I see. Well, let me ask you a question," I said.

"What?" she asked.

"If we got married, would you change your name?"

"Ty, we are not getting married, so why would you ask me that?"

"Just entertain me. Would you change your name?"

"What do you mean, 'would I change my name'?"

"Would you be Porchia Williams or Porchia Gamble?"

"Mrs. Porchia Gamble of course. Why?"

"Just wondering. So what's up?"

"I read something in The *Gossip* about you."

"Yeah, my sperm donor died, and I went to the funeral."

"You did what?"

"Yeah, I went to the funeral."

"I thought you did not want to have anything to do with him or his family."

"Porchia, I met my sister. She is the sweetest little girl. I fell in love with her at first sight."

"Really? Well, that is great. I am proud of you Mr. Gamble. So did you hear about Raheem?"

"Yeah, I heard that was in the same edition," I said.

"I hope that Jinn is okay. Did you ever get a chance to speak with her?" Porchia asked.

"No, I did not. But I am certain she has tested herself by now."

"Ty, I don't understand how he could do that to Jinn. They were married."

"Well, you know Raheem doesn't love anyone but Raheem."

"Well, I pray that he heals and learns to really love himself. If he truly loved himself, he would love others also," she said.

"Yeah. So how is school going?"

"It's a challenge, but I am loving it. It has challenged, not only my way of living and thinking, but the manner in which I exist and co-exist with others."

"I am happy for you. And your call has been really timely."

"Why? What's going on?" she asked.

"Nothing is going on now. You have made certain of that."

"Okay, Ty. I have no idea what you are talking about. But if I helped with this call, I was led by God. You were on my mind, and I wanted to let you know."

"Well, thank you. I appreciate it. I love you," I confessed.

"You are welcome. I love you, too. Take care."

"I will," I said and held the phone by my heart for a while.

I walked out of the jewelry store and back to the hotel. When I walked back in, Jill was smiling. She ran up to me and said, "I can't wait for us to exchange our vows. I will make you a very happy man for the rest of your life."

I just stared at her, and she asked with a very concerned look, "What happened?"

"Jill, you are beautiful, and you have more appealing attributes than almost any woman I have ever met, but I can't do this."

"What do you mean 'you can't do this'? I just went out and bought a wedding dress!"

"I will pay you for the dress."

"You got me in Vegas, all excited to marry you, and then you come back and say that we are not going to get married! That is bullshit. We are going to get married TODAY!"

"But, Jill, we don't even know each other well enough. I didn't even know your name or that you wanted to keep your maiden name."

"I want to keep my name because I am professionally established under that name. I can't change my name now."

"I am certain people will know who you are if you hyphenated your name."

"Is this what this is all about? You don't want to marry me because I don't want to change my name? Well, dammit, I will hyphenate my name if that is what it's gonna take."

"No, I think we need to get to know each other and have a proper wedding with our family and friends."

"Ty, I don't need all the fanfare. I don't have any family, do you? And don't you get enough fanfare on and off the court?"

"Answer me this Jill. Why do you want to marry me?"

"Answer me this Ty. Why should I not want to marry you?"

I stared at her a minute and thought, Porchia does not want me, but Jill sure would look good on my arms, and even more importantly, maybe men would stop making sexual advances toward me if I married her. I, then, said, "Okay, if you are sure, let's do it."

She ran and hugged me and said, "I will be the best wife in the world."

"I will hold you to that, Ms. Merlino, soon to be Mrs. Merlino-Gamble."

"All right, already, Ty. I said I would change my last name!"

She then told me I would have to leave the room and go to another room she'd booked for me because I could not see her wedding dress.

"So you are kicking me out of our room already?"

"Not kicking you out, just putting you on ice until you see me walking down the aisle."

I took the room card key from her and retreated to the other room. I realized that I had not found rings, so I called the concierge and asked him to send a jeweler to my room as soon as possible. Within twenty minutes, a woman showed up with a case. She showed me several rings, and I picked the one I thought that Jill would appreciate.

I really did not know what Jill liked, but I noticed that she liked to stand out, so I got her a twenty-four karat yellow-gold ring with a six carat princess-cut solitaire diamond, which was surrounded by two one-carat diamonds on each side, accompanied by a single twenty-four karat band. I picked out a simple band with four one-carat diamonds surrounding the band for myself. I was not crazy about gold, but I noticed that Jill wore more yellow gold than white gold or platinum. Right after I completed the ring transaction, the tailor came in with several suits. I chose a champagne-colored tuxedo with a coral cummerbund, a white tuxedo shirt, and a coral bow tie.

Chapter 25

I anxiously waited in the chapel for my bride. When Jill walked in, I almost fell out. She had on a strapless, backless dress. It also had cut outs on the sides. The flesh-colored dress fit snuggly at her hips and flared at the bottom. It hugged her booty like a BMW hugs curves. My heart started beating so fast, I thought I would pass out. I don't know if it was from the excitement of seeing her looking so sexy, or from me being afraid that I was making the biggest mistake in my life. Whatever it was, I hoped that she made it down the aisle before I passed out.

I did not choose the traditional wedding song; instead I chose Jagged Edge's "Let's Get Married" since it was fitting for us, with the exception that we had not known each other for a long time. Hell, we barely knew each other, but we both agreed that we would meet down the aisle and get to know each other after we married. While standing there watching her walk down the aisle to the song, I briefly thought that if it were Porchia I was marrying, I would have chosen "Ribbon in the Sky" for her to walk down the aisle to.

I had also chosen non-traditional vows that concentrated more on taking paths in life where we supported each other through the journey. Not once did we mention love because we had not gotten to that point yet. But our vows included attributes that we would like to carry on in our partnership, such as honesty, sharing, laughter, compassion, and understanding. When the preacher pronounced us partners in marriage, I leaned over, and Jill took over the kiss and kissed me like she had not kissed a man in ten years. When she finally let me go, I was gasping for air. I thought, *If this is the kiss, what will the sex be like?* I hoped that she did not turn into Lisa on me because I was not certain I had that type of energy to contribute on a daily basis.

Before I could get ready to conjugate my marriage to my wife, Coc called me and said, "Man, tell me that you got a prenup?"

I looked at Jill and said I needed to take this call and walked into the media room.

"You heard already?"

"Man, it is my job to protect your assets. You got married and did not get a prenup? Have you lost your mind?"

"I did not even think about it. But she does not need my money."

"Look. You may be right. She may not need your money, but she will be entitled to half of your earnings when you divorce."

"We are not going to divorce," I said.

"You don't even know this chick, Ty!"

"So how did you find out?"

"You did not get a private marriage license. And I get information on all my clients as soon as something life-changing happens."

"You spy on me?"

"No, I protect you!"

"Well, I don't appreciate you coming at me like this, man. I know what I am doing."

"I guess the pussy is that good, huh?"

"You are out of line. We can discuss this later."

"I will draw up a post-nuptial agreement. And your job will be to get her to sign it."

"We will discuss this later. My wife is waiting for me."

"Yeah, probably waiting to get all of your money."

"You're acting as if she is taking your money."

"When she takes your money, she IS taking my money. Call me as soon as you get her to sign that prenup."

"We'll talk later!" I said as I angrily hung up the phone.

I could not believe I did not think of a pre-nuptial agreement. I knew Coc was right. Hell, I had tried to get out of the marriage, but because Jill was hyped, I went through with it. I knew that our lives would be an adventure. But I was ready for it. I knew I would have to, somehow, break the news to Porchia about the marriage because I did not want her to read about it. I also made a note to call Aunt Verdie and Poo Man.

When I walked back into the parlor, Jill was not there. I called out her name, and she said, "I am in here, husband." Her voice came from the bedroom, and when I walked in, she was on the bed wearing a red negligee and red stilettos, laying on her stomach with her feet in the air. This lady had pulled out all the stops to make certain she gave me a rise. And rise was exactly what happened. I had a lot to work with, and I hoped she was ready for it since she'd told me she had not had sex in two years. I stripped off my clothes and straddled my wife and asked her whether she was ready for all this.

She said, while groping my dick, "I have been waiting my entire life for all of this."

I took my time kissing her entire back, then moved down to her ass. And what an ass she had. I kissed her ass, then parted her ass and ran my tongue down her crack. She moaned softly. I started teasing her hole with my tongue. She moaned a little louder. I then darted my tongue in and out of her ass, and she started screaming to the point that she scared me. I stopped and asked her if she was okay. She told me that it felt good. I continued kissing her down the back of her legs.

When I got to her feet, I kissed her feet and sucked her toes. She started shaking violently. I thought that maybe she was having a seizure, so I stopped again and asked her if she was okay. She was breathing hard and said, "I am just enjoying it all." I then turned her over and began kissing her. She was panting hard to the point it seemed like she was having difficulty breathing. So I moved down to her neck, and when I kissed her in the middle of her neck, she started trembling. I moved down to her breasts and gently licked her nipples.

She said, "I can't take anymore. Please give it to me."

I asked her seductively, "What do you want me to give to you?"

"Your eleven-inch dick."

"It is eleven and a half inches, and I am not certain you are ready for it."

I sucked her nipples, and she moaned again. I moved down to her stomach and played with her navel. I took my tongue and swirled it around a couple of times, and she began moaning again. I then went down and found that she was completely shaven. That seemed to make my dick even harder. I began kissing her pussy and eventually started playing with her clit. I opened up her lips and gently put my tongue between them. I played around until I found her spot because she began wiggling and moaning. I backed up and went down to her hole, which was juicy and wet. I sucked her, and she moaned loudly again. I eased up and went down to her knees, and she said, "No! That will make me cum!"

I slid back up and found her spot on her clit. I licked and sucked, as she screamed like she was getting murdered and began squirting up the room. My face and the bed were covered with her juices. It looked as if she had squirted all the way to the headboard. After she finished her two-minute episode, she looked at me and said, "Why did you do that?"

I looked and said, "Isn't that the point?"

She said, "But I was not ready to cum?"

I looked at her and said, "And I am not done making you cum."

I touched her, and she was still wet. For the first time, I would be entering someone without a condom. When I entered her, it felt like velvet covered my shaft. She was tight, but soft and silky. I started off slowly, playing with her with the head of my dick. I slowly put all of me in her, and she began moaning. I stroked her deeply and slowly. I could feel her getting wetter as her pussy embraced my dick. It was getting good to me, so I sped up my strokes, and she moaned loudly. I went in harder and deeper as she yelled at the top of her voice. She made all sorts of crazy sounds while yelling. I then heard knocks on the door and someone yelling, "This is security! Is everything okay in there?"

I shouted, "We good!"

At the same time, the phone rang. I answered it, and the voice on the line said, "Mr. Gamble, is everything okay?"

"Yes, it is."

"Sir, we received several phone calls that there may be a disturbance in your room."

"No. Everything is fine. I apologize for the noise."

"No problem, sir. Glad that you are okay. Let us know if you need anything."

"I will. Thank you again."

I hung up the phone and looked at Jill and said, "So you are a yeller, I see."

She looked at me apologetically and said, "I am sorry Ty. I told you it had been a long time. Did you cum yet?"

"No, I have not."

She then pushed me back on the bed and started licking my dick as if it was an ice cream cone. I thought, *I hope this is not the way that my woman will give me head!* She then went down to my balls and started licking it the same way she had licked my dick. I stopped her and said, "Baby, this is not going to make me cum."

"Let me know how you like it," she said with a concerned look on her face.

"Never mind, baby. I am going to take a shower." I left the bed disappointed.

Chapter 26

I jumped in the shower, hoping to take the edge off. I soaped up my dick and started stroking it. I was having no luck, so I started thinking about how beautiful my wife looked laying in her red negligee. That did not help, so I thought about me and Lisa having wild sex. That helped a little. Then, I thought about Raheem banging my ass, just the way I liked it. I got little more excited, but still did not cum. Then, I pictured Porchia smiling at me with her beautiful eyes, saying something sassy, and I started shooting all over the place. I let out a moan of relief and smiled.

When I got out of the shower, Jill was standing there. She apologized for both yelling and not making me cum. I told her that it was all right; she would have plenty of time to make it up. She was looking very disappointed, so I reached over and kissed her passionately. I felt myself rising again, but I stopped, just in case she was not ready to engage in sex again.

She looked at me and said, "I want to make you happy."

I looked at her and said, "You already have."

I knew that I was not telling the truth and already breaking my vow about being honest, but I knew that she needed to feel supported, which I also promised to do as part of our vows. I was not yet certain how to deal with this dichotomy, but I was certain this would make an interesting subject during my next session with Dr. Mouton. I thought that the raw honesty that I'd shared with Dr. Mouton might now be compromised since I had married his business partner.

As I continued drying myself off, I started thinking that my nickname for Jill should be Ol' Yeller, and began smiling. I hoped that what happened in the bedroom was not going to be indicative of our entire relationship. It is not my idea of good sex to make my wife cum, while I jacked-off thinking about ex-lovers in the shower.

She looked at me and asked me what I was thinking about. I told her, "Nothing."

She got up close to me and looked me directly in my eyes and said, "Look. We did not start this marriage with lies. So let's not mess up a good thing."

I looked at her and smiled and said, "I was just thinking about you yelling in bed."

"Oh, so that was funny to you?"

"Yes, it was hilarious."

"Well, how about me making you yell next time big guy?"

"I have never yelled in bed, Mrs. Merlino-Gamble."

"Well, when we get home, I will have a surprise for you."

"Oh, so why do I have to wait until we get home?" I asked.

"Because patience is a virtue, Mr. Gamble," she said.

I asked Jill to dry off my back and thought about home and asked, "So are you moving in with me?"

She looked at me confused and said, "I thought, perhaps, you could move in with me."

"I guess those are some of the small things we did not consider," I said and laughed.

"Well, that is not exactly small. See my dad bought me the house, and that is the only tie I have to him. I don't want to move out of my house."

That was when I realized that I probably should have thought about this marriage more before just flying to Vegas to tie the knot, especially to someone that I did not know or love.

"So, Jill, will you call your mother and let her know that you got married?"

"I have not spoken to my mother in three years. She remarried another man from a rival family about a month after my dad was found floating in the lake. I can only assume that she was cheating on him. Hell, for all I know, she may have had him killed. I was never really close to her anyway. I was always a daddy's girl."

That was when I realized I had just married a dead mobster's daughter. I then asked, "Well, do you have any other brothers or sisters?"

"No, I was the only child and the apple of my daddy's eye."

"Well, I have a few people to call. The media might get a hold of the story, and I would like to tell them before that happens."

"So is one of them going to be Porchia?"

"Yes, one of them is going to be Porchia."

"Should I be jealous?"

I walked over to her and lied to her again and said, "No, beautiful wife. You have absolutely no reason to be jealous."

She kissed me on my lips and said, "I will make you a very happy husband."

I kissed her on her neck and said, "I will spend every day enjoying you making me a very happy husband, Mrs. Merlino-Gamble."

She then said, "There is one person I need to call."

"Should I be jealous?" I asked.

"Hmm … I don't think so, but you may need to find another therapist."

"Yeah, I had been thinking about that, too." I patted her on her juicy, round ass and said, "Hurry and shower, so we can go out to dinner and finish brainstorming about how we will live, where we will live, and who we will tell."

I did not feel like going out of the hotel, so I made a private room reservation at a restaurant located within the hotel. Our meal was so spectacular that I had to meet the head chef and give him my personal kudos. I was surprised to find out that he was a brother. I smiled and told him it was an honor to meet him. He told me in return that his name was Jeremy, that he was my number one fan, and the honor was all his.

I introduced Jill as my wife, and he kissed her hand. He then told me that he would appreciate an autograph. I took my linen napkin and wrote out a personal autograph to him. When I handed him the napkin, he touched my hand in an odd manner and gave me a flirtatious smile and said, "Thank you."

I thought, I am here with my wife, and they are still coming on to me. Jill must have read my mind because she said, "Yeah, I saw that," and smiled.

We were surprised with a dessert that looked absolutely delicious, but I passed because I knew that I had already overdone it. Jill devoured it within minutes. I wondered how she kept her body looking so amazing because each time I had dined with her she enjoyed a hefty meal and dessert. She looked at me as if she read my mind and said, "Perhaps we need to retire to our room, so I can work these calories off."

I told her that I would love to, but I had to take care of business before I did anything else.

She looked at me and said, "Well, in that case, I will go and change to work out."

I smiled at her and said, "Yes, work it on out because I will leave you if you get fat."

"Well, I am planning on getting fat soon, because I need a little Gamble bambino running around the house."

"And which house will that be, Mrs. Merlino-Gamble?"

She got up, leaned over, kissed me, and said, "We will work that one out real soon, Mr. Gamble."

After she left, I pulled out my phone and looked at it. How was I going to tell Porchia what I'd just done? I knew that I had to before the media took the story and ran with it, especially since Jill was a mobster's daughter. I could see the headlines now: "Ty Gamble Marries Mobster's Daughter." I thought about different angles to put on the story, but when I got the nerve to call her and she answered, I blurted out, "Pocahontas, I just fucked up!"

I told her the story, and she just remained silent the entire time. I had to ask her several times whether she was still there. I paused and asked her again whether she was still there. She responded, "Ty, marriage is a union that should not be taken lightly. It is one of the things that God holds in high regard. In Hebrews 13:4, it says, 'Let marriage be held in honor among all, and let the marriage bed be undefiled, for God will judge the sexually immoral and adulterous.' My plea to you is that you honor the vows of your marriage. Please let this be the last time you contact me."

And then I heard silence. I said, "Pocahontas, are you there?"

I knew from the sound of her voice that I had lost her forever. I sat there and cried like a baby.

The chef came in and said, "Can I help you with anything?"

I needed someone to talk with at that time. So I looked at him and said, "Man, I just fucked up!"

He said, "You don't look good at all. You would not want anyone to see you like this. Come. You can take time to get yourself together in my office."

He led me through some hallways and into the service elevator. We went up a couple of floors until we reached what looked like a suite. He opened it up, and I could see a big desk. I was an emotional wreck, so I went immediately and sat on the oversized sectional sofa. I put my hands in my face and just started crying again. Jeremy handed me some tissue and said, "Do you want to talk about it?"

As I shook my head, Jeremy got on his knees and reached for my waist. I looked at him and said, "Man, what the fuck are you doing?"

"Trying to make you feel better."

He touched my dick, and I guess he felt it stiffen because he smiled as he unbuttoned and unzipped my jeans. The next thing I knew; my dick was sticking straight out of my jeans.

Jeremy sucked me until I forgot why I was crying and until I was screaming like Jill. I burst, looked at him and said, "Dayuum, man, you had me screaming like a bitch! Do you have somewhere I can go clean up?"

He pointed to his right and said, "Yeah, the bathroom is right around the corner."

I got up and went into the bathroom, thinking, *Damn, I have not been married twenty-four hours. Porchia is making me cry, and this dude I don't even know is making me scream.* I knew, at that moment, that I had made the biggest mistake of my life. What the hell was I thinking when I married Jill? After pissing and cleaning up, I sat on the toilet, thinking about what I could do to get out of the mess I'd just created.

Chapter 27

I missed a call from Coc, informing me that Essence wanted to list me as one of its most eligible bachelors, and he wanted to know how he should respond to their request. I was packing when Jill entered the room and said, "I guess the honeymoon is over."

I looked at her and lied, "Yeah, some issues came up with the non-profit, and I need to meet with Coc and Bart right away. But you are welcome to stay."

"How dare you say that to your newly married wife? I go where my hubby goes. What time does our plane leave?"

"I have not made reservations yet. I thought maybe you wanted to catch some of the conference that you were attending in Houston. And I need to go to Atlanta," I said.

"I can go to Atlanta with you," Jill said, "unless you have other plans."

"No. I don't have other plans. And don't start acting like a jealous wife on day one," I said, half-joking.

"You just seem different from when I left you at dinner."

"Yeah, I spoke with Porchia."

"Well, was everything okay?"

"No, it was not. But it will be okay."

"Is there anything you would like to talk about?"

"No, and you don't have to play Dr. Merlino-Gamble with me?"

"Okay. Just checking. Well, I need to take another shower after this workout. Do you think we could leave tomorrow?"

"Let me call the airline and see what is available."

I did not want to stay another night in Vegas, so I knew I would do anything I could to get out tonight. I picked up the phone to have the concierge make reservations for us to leave and my phone rang. I answered it, and all I heard was crying.

"Hello. Who is this?" I asked.

No answer, just crying.

"Hello!" I said again.

Then the caller said, "Hello, Brother. It's me."

"Penny! Baby, what's wrong?"

"Mommy got into an accident, and she has gone to heaven with Daddy."

"Baby, what are you saying?"

"Can you come get me?"

"Sweetie, where are you?"

"I am with Mammy."

I knew that is what she called Ms. Eurice's mother who was about ninety years old.

"Can I speak with Mammy?"

Penny yelled for her grandmother. Her grandmother came to the phone and said, "Hello."

I did not remember her grandmother's name, so I said, "Hi, Mammy. This is Ty. What happened?"

Mammy told me that Eurice was killed in a car accident and that Penny had been crying for me ever since it happened. I told Mammy I would be there as soon as possible. I immediately called Coc and told him what had happened and to look into seeing who would be caring for Penny. I called the concierge and told him that I needed two first-class, one-way tickets to Houston. When Jill came out of the shower, she looked at me and asked, "What's wrong?"

I told her about what happened, and she seemed even more upset than I was. The concierge called back and said that he'd booked our flights for 8:07 a.m. and asked me whether that time would work. I asked him whether that was the earliest, and he told me that it was. I sat on the bed in disbelief. The last twenty-four hours of my life seemed to be spinning out of control.

At least, I was too preoccupied to have sex with my new wife. She seemed to be just as preoccupied as I was. When we finally laid down for the night, she told me she needed to discuss something with me. I asked her if it was a heavy discussion, perhaps it could wait until morning. She said it was heavy, but she wanted to discuss it tonight. I realized then that marriage would be a lot more difficult than I thought. I never had to talk about anything I did not want to talk about with anyone before, not even my mother. I turned over and gave Jill my complete attention.

"What do you think about us taking Penny to live with us?"

"I am not certain how that would work. I plan on making certain she is provided for, but I don't think I can physically take care of her."

"Together, we can. I know when the season starts, life will be crazy. But I could adjust my schedule, so I can be there for her before and after school. And we could hire a nanny to help."

"I don't know Jill. I have never taken care of a child before. The most I have done is play with my little cousins for a hot minute. I don't think I am ready to be a full-time daddy just yet."

"Ty, you would make a great parental figure. And you know that little girl is so sweet. She would not be much trouble at all."

I was really confused now. I was thinking about how I could get rid of Jill, and now she was trying to strap me with a child. I told her that Coc was looking into who would take care of Penny, and we could discuss it after we received that information. That seemed to please Jill because she reached over and kissed me, smiled, and said, "You are the greatest husband a wife could ask for Ty."

If only she knew that I was thinking about how to get out of the marriage, and that my dick had been in another man's mouth not that long ago.

****

When we landed in Houston, I checked my calls and found out that Coc had left me a message asking me to return his call. I decided that I would rent a car to take Jill to meet Aunt Verdie, then call him from there.

When we walked into Aunt Verdie's, she was stinking up the house cooking. I ran straight for the pot. When I put my hand on the top, she slapped my hand away and said, "Boy, you know your mama taught you better than that. You don't go into the kitchen without washing your hands. And where are your manners? Are you gonna introduce me to your friend!"

"My bad Auntie. I smelled that good cooking and got all excited. Aunt Verdie, this is my wife, Jill."

Aunt Verdie looked at me with that "what-did-you-say-Willis" look and said, "Boy, did you just say wife?"

"Yes, ma'am."

She ran to Jill, grabbed her, kissed her, and said, "How you doin' baby? Wow! You got a tall one there. Do you play basketball too?"

"I'm fine ma'am. No, I'm just a fan of both the game and my very talented husband. It does smell good in here ma'am."

"Oh no, I ain't no ma'am. I'm Aunt Verdie. I'm cooking some red beans and hammocks."

Jill looked confused and said, "Hammocks?"

"Yeah, baby. You ain't neva heard of hammocks? Where you from?"

"I grew up in Philly."

"Y'all don't cook with hammocks in Philly?"

"Well, my mom did not cook a lot when I was growing up. Luisa made most of our meals, and it was usually Italian food."

"Oh, baby, you don't look Italian. You look just like my cousin Freda."

"Yes, ma'am. Oops, I'm sorry, I mean Aunt Verdie. I'm half-Italian."

"Well, you will fit right in with us, baby. But you gonna have to try my hammocks."

"I can't wait to try them," Jill said while smiling at Aunt Verdie.

"Auntie, where is Poo Man?" I asked.

"He got a job working as an offshoreman. He didn't tell you?"

"No, and I just spoke to him. How long has he been working?"

"He just left last night. I think he told me he would be out there for fourteen days. Then come back for five days."

"Does he still have his place?"

"Yeah, he wants to keep his apartment. Where else would he live when he came home? You know that boy can't live with me! Speaking of staying, how long y'all staying? You always think you too fancy to stay with me now. You know you don't have to get a hotel!"

"I just came down to see my sister. Her mother was killed in a car accident last night, and she called me crying and asked for me to come."

"What? Baby, I am sorry to hear that! So how long will you be here?"

"I don't know yet, but I need to make a call to find out some things from my lawyer."

I looked at Jill and asked her if she would be okay if I stepped into the back room to make a few calls.

Aunt Verdie looked at me and said, "Go on, boy! I ain't gonna bite her."

I laughed, kissed Aunt Verdie, then Jill, and said, "I will be back shortly."

I returned Coc's call, and he told me that there was nobody suitable to take care of Penny. Her mother's family were all on welfare, drugs, or both. Her brothers were in and out of jail, and her grandmother was old with failing health. I told Coc to take the necessary steps for me to get guardianship over Penny. He said that it should not be difficult because I was the closet next of kin. I sat there shaking my head at how life could turn on a dime. I wanted, more than anything, to share this with Porchia, but knew that she would probably not take my call.

I walked back into the kitchen to find Jill with a big ol' hammock in her mouth, tearing it up. I laughed and said, "Now, this is a Kodak moment."

She looked at me, smiling, and said, "I would just say, as all you men say, it wasn't me."

I watched her talking and having a good time with Aunt Verdie and knew that she was a good woman because Aunt Verdie could smell a fake a mile away. She would have pulled me aside and insisted that I end the marriage and would have told me things like my mama was turning over in her grave. I, somehow, wished that was the case. I knew at that moment, it would be it would be impossible for me to leave Jill.

I started thinking about my life and started trying to put things in perspective. I left Birmingham to attend the funeral of a man I did not know, and I would return to Birmingham with a wife and a child. I knew that my entire life had to change because now I would be responsible for two people. When it came to Jill, I was not that afraid because I knew that Jill could take care of herself. But with Penny, she was only a child, and she would require proper care and nurturing, which I was not sure I was prepared or equipped to provide. I had been accustomed to making decisions based on what I wanted. Now there was a little one who required me to act with her best interest in mind, and a wife that expected me to consider her best interest also.

Chapter 28

Jill and I spent one night with Aunt Verdie, then drove to Beaumont for a couple of days and stayed at my mom's house. After my mom's death, I'd hired individuals to check on the house, clean it, and cut the lawn. When we arrived, the home looked as if someone lived there. I rarely went there because it reminded me so much of my mom. I had not changed anything in the house. Jill fell in love with the house and said that we should visit more often. She said that she felt a warm presence and adored the coziness of the home. I knew that it was my mom's way of welcoming Jill.

I decided that, since I had not seen or spoken with Magrand in a while, that we would go and visit her. She did not seem excited about meeting my wife, and she was even less excited about the news of us taking guardianship of Penny. Magrand was never really supportive of any of the things that I did, including playing professional ball. I was okay with her attitude, because that only meant that I would not feel obligated to bring Jill or Penny around her. I believed Penny only served as a reminder of my sperm donor to her. Magrand never forgave my mother for moving away and living with a man whom she never married, then having an illegitimate child with him. Nonetheless, I wanted to keep my mom's wishes of staying close to family, but I felt the only real family I had was Aunt Verdie and Poo Man.

Coc took care of all the paperwork that we needed to obtain complete guardianship over Penny. Afterward, we went to pick her up from Mammy's. She was so happy to see us that she was talking a mile per minute. Mammy said she had her clothes packed and waiting for us to pick her up for two days. She kissed Mammy and ran to us and said, "Ok. I am ready for my new life." She waved to her grandmother before getting in the car, smiled, and said, "I love you, Mammy, and will be in touch soon. Smooches!"

From my observations, I knew that Penny was going to be more than a handful.

Within a couple of hours, Jill had planned out the rest of our lives. She decided that she wanted to fulfill the role as primary care provider for Penny, so she would move in with me because the school district was better where I lived. She also decided to substantially reduce her hours at work, so she could properly care for Penny. Jill informed me that she had registered Penny for a dance class with one of her friends. She also told me that she would look into music and acting classes when we returned. She said, although the school district where I lived was excellent, perhaps she should also look into private schooling for Penny. I allowed her to do all the planning she liked because, frankly, I was overwhelmed by it all.

Penny was an amazing little girl. She acted as if she had been riding planes all of her life. She was extra excited when she met the pilots; especially when she found out the co-pilot was a female. When the female co-pilot gave her some wings, she looked at me with her big eyes and said, "Brother, maybe one day I can be a pilot, and I can fly you to your games."

As I laughed out loudly and thought about all the money I had spent in the last few months on airline tickets, I thought, *It would be great to have a personal plane and pilot.*

The flight attendants catered to every one of Penny's needs. By the time we landed, she had made friends with all of the flight attendants, and a few of the passengers. It was so nice to see the innocence that she displayed with others. She was so pure and trusting; I knew that I would have to make certain she was protected from predators like Rico. As I watched her sleep on the plane, I knew that I would do anything to protect her from the cruelness of the world.

I thought back to my mom on her death bed, apologizing for not recognizing that I was being abused by Rico. Now I understood that her pain was not necessarily associated with what happened, but more so with her not knowing that it was happening. I realized that a parent should be aware of, at all times, what was happening with his or her child.

When we arrived in Birmingham, Jill asked that we drop her off at her house, so she could get some of her things together before coming to my house. She told me that she would be over within the next few hours. Jill was captivating my heart as I watched how she interacted with Penny. I realized that she would be easy to fall in love with. When I brought her bags to her door, I told her that I was glad I'd found her. She told me, in return, that she was glad that she'd chosen me.

We drove to my house, and when we pulled up, Penny's eyes became really big, and she said, "Brother, is this where you live?"

I answered, "No Princess, this is where we live."

She ran out of the car around the large driveway, screaming, "I really feel like a princess now because I will be living in a castle!"

I could not do anything but laugh. Once we got into the house, she ran to all of the rooms to check them out. When she got to the living room she asked if she could play the piano. I told her that she needed to pick out what room she wanted upstairs first. She ran up the stairs before I could get all of the luggage in the house. I heard her shouting, "I want this one!"

By the time I arrived, she was claiming my room as her own.

"No, Princess. This is the one room that you can't have. This is mine."

She looked a little sad for a minute, then started running to all of the other rooms. She eventually picked the room overlooking the pool. That was the one room that looked a little unwelcoming and cold to me, but it had a lovely view of the grounds. I knew that Jill would have some ideas on how to redecorate it for a little girl. Penny looked at me and asked, "Can I go swimming?"

I was amazed that she had already forgotten about playing the piano. I told her that we needed to get settled in before she could go swimming. I wondered whether she even knew how to swim. I realized that there was a lot that I would have to learn about Penny. *Did she have any allergies? What foods did she like? Did she sleep with the lights on or off?* I started feeling a lot of anxiety about being a guardian and wished that Jill was already here, so she could give me ideas on what we should do first.

Penny interrupted my thoughts and said, "Brother, I am hungry. Are we going to eat?"

"Yes we will. Do you like McDonald's?"

My cooking skills were limited to gumbo, and I definitely did not know anything about cooking for a child or what they liked to eat.

"No, Mommy would not let me eat at McDonald's. She always said that type of food was not good for me or my soul," Penny said with a serious look on her face.

"Well Princess, what do you like?"

"I like homemade turkey burgers."

I thought about calling Ms. Blanchard, who doubled as my housekeeper and cook. But I knew that Penny probably needed to eat right away. I caught her hand and said, "Let's go see what we can hook up."

When we went to the kitchen, I searched and searched and got Penny to agree on a TSPBJ, a Ty's Special Peanut Butter and Jelly Sandwich. Penny swore that it was the best sandwich she had ever had in her life. I wondered whether Jill knew how to cook. If not, I would have to hone up on my skills or hire a nanny with mad cooking skills.

Penny talked all through dinner, while my mind raced on things like getting her registered for school. The kids were almost out of school for their summer break, but I knew that there was some process to get them into school, but I was not quite certain what that was. I also wrestled with the fact that she had suffered a lot of trauma with the deaths of both of her parents, and she probably needed counseling. I knew Jill could definitely help with finding the right person for Penny. She seemed like she was a well-adjusted child, but I knew that losing her mother was something that no child should have to deal with alone.

Penny and I were about to go upstairs to get her room together when my phone rang. It was my brother Tyrone. He wanted to know why I had taken his little sister away. He reminded me that he had warned me to stay away from his family. He told me that they did not want anything to do with me. He went on to say that he was going to get Penny back and that I had no right to take her away from the only family she knew. He went on to inform me that he would normally take this to the streets, but this time he would take it to the courts. I did not do much talking, I just listened because I did not want to upset Penny.

When I heard enough of his ranting, I ended the conversation with, "I will see you in court."

When I got off the phone, Penny looked at me and said, "What's wrong Brother?"

"Nothing for you to worry about Princess. Are you ready to unpack?"

"Yes, I guess so."

"Would you prefer to do something else?"

"Yes, I would. Can I play some games?" she asked.

I thought maybe that would be good for her since she'd had a very long day, so I said, "Sure, you can play for a little while. While you play, I will take care of business."

She looked at me and asked, "Brother, would you like me to help you with your business?"

I smiled at her and said, "No Princess, I can handle it. You have fun."

She looked up at me with her beautiful, big, brown, innocent eyes and said, "Thanks. You are the best big brother ever."

"And you are the sweetest little sister ever." I bent down and kissed her on her forehead.

After she ran upstairs, I called Jill to find out how much longer she would be. She did not answer her phone, so I left her a message asking her to call me back as soon as she could. I then called Ms. Blanchard to discuss with her adding additional hours to her schedule for cleaning and cooking. I explained that I had taken custody of my little sister and that we would need, at least, three balanced and nutritional meals prepared during the day. She stated that she could easily fit that into her schedule. I asked her whether she had any referrals for a nanny. I proceeded to rattle off the skills I desired. She assured me that she would provide me with a couple of names when she came in the next day.

After speaking with Ms. Blanchard, I called Coc to tell him about the conversation I'd had with Tyrone. After I finished an hour-long conversation with Coc, I called Bart to get an update on what was happening with Rising Above. I was tired of talking after I finished my conversation with Bart, so I took a break to check on Penny. She was on my PlayStation 4 playing Assassins. I did not think this was a good idea for her to be playing that game, but I did not have any kid-friendly games for her to play. So I sat by her and watched her play. I took a mental note to find some acceptable children games.

I suddenly realized it was late, and I still had not heard from Jill. I called her number again, and there was no answer. When I told Penny that it was time for bed, she begged me to stay up a little longer to wait on Jill. I knew that I would have to set boundaries for her, but I also did not want to come down too hard on her right now. So I told her that she could wait on Jill for one more hour; but if Jill was not home within the hour, she would have to take a bath and go to bed. She started playing Mortal Combat and was pretty good at it. I asked if she had played these games before. She told me that Tyrone had a PS4 and that he would play them with her, and when he was not around, she played by herself.

I stepped away to call Dr. Mouton, but he failed to answer his phone also. I left him a message letting him know that I was looking for Jill, and I asked that, if he saw her, to ask her to call me right away. I realized I did not know Jill at all if she could just leave me hanging like this. I wondered, *Why did I insist on marrying this lady so quickly?*

Chapter 29

I fell asleep in the media room waiting for Jill and woke up at three o'clock in the morning. I looked at my phone and had not received a call. I called Terry and asked him to come over to watch Penny. He protested at first, telling me that he was a driver, not a babysitter. I tried to convince him that she was fast asleep and that I would be back before he knew it. I got tired of his whining and did not want play no games, so I said, "If you want to keep your job, I would advise you to get yo' trifling azz over here right now!"

When Terry pulled up, I ran out and told him I would be back as soon as possible. I wondered what type of head game Jill was pulling. She pretended to be very interested in me, and even more so in Penny. I could not believe that she had not called or shown up. I would have a few choice words for her and papers ready for an annulment by early morning.

By the time I pulled up to her house and saw her car sitting in the driveway, I was ready to kill a bitch. I knew I had to calm down before going into her house.

I walked up to the door and rang the doorbell. When there was no answer, I began banging on the door and yelling Jill's name. I tried to open the door, and it opened right up. I never understood why people did not lock their doors. Even when living in what was considered a safe neighborhood, I knew it was never wise to leave the door unlocked. I thought that Jill was perhaps not as bright as I had given her credit for. On second thought, I concluded that maybe she was in a rush to pack and was trying to run in and out of her house quickly. At that moment, my emotions changed from anger to concern.

When I walked through the door, I yelled, "Jill!"

I closed the door and locked it and yelled Jill's name again because I did not want her to think I was an intruder. Still, there was no answer. I was not familiar with Jill's house. To the left was a formal living room and to the right was a doorway that led to the kitchen. Jill was not there. I screamed out her name again as I opened the door that led to the backyard, there was no Jill. I began running from room to room screaming her name. I made it to the master bedroom, and I could see that she'd started packing because clothes were sprawled out everywhere. I ran into the bathroom and found Jill lying on the floor.

I went to her to pick her up and asked, "Jill, are you okay?"

She did not respond. I picked her up off the floor and placed her on the bed. Then I dialed 911 and told them that I'd found my wife lying on the bathroom floor, unresponsive. They asked me for the address and I gave it to them. They asked me what happened, and I told them I did not know because I had just arrived.

After the paramedics arrived and examined her, one of them came over and said, "I am so sorry."

I lost consciousness when the paramedic said those words.

When I woke up, I was lying on a strange sofa in a strange house. Then I remembered what happened. I looked up and saw Dr. Mouton and said, "How is Jill?"

Dr. Mouton sat next to me, put his arm on my shoulder, and said, "She's gone."

"What do you mean she's gone?"

"She is dead."

I stared at Dr. Mouton and said, "But we just got married!"

"Yeah, I know. She called me from Vegas."

"What happened?"

"I don't know. After I picked up your message and attempted to call her several times and there was no answer, I decided to come check on her. The paramedics had you lying on the sofa, but they were taking her body away when I arrived. The police are here to question you. I think you should get an attorney."

"For what?"

"They look at the people closest to the victim first."

"I would never hurt Jill. She was on the floor when I arrived. I moved her to the bed and called 911."

"I believe you. But you still need to protect yourself."

I looked at Dr. Mouton, rubbed my head and said, "This can't be happening!"

He got up and came back with a bottle of water. "Would you like some water?"

As I began drinking the water, the detective came in and said, "Mr. Gamble, we need you to come with us to the station for questioning."

"Am I under arrest officer?"

"No, we just need to find out what happened."

"I don't need to go to the station to tell you what happened. I can tell you right now. I came here and found my wife lying on the bathroom floor!"

"Mr. Gamble, I assure you, it would be best to come to the station. We will have some follow-up questions for you."

"Should I get an attorney?"

"You can get an attorney if you'd like, but you are not a suspect. We are just trying to figure out what happened."

Dr. Mouton convinced the officer that it was best to allow him to drive me to the police station. Before leaving for the station, I called Terry to tell him what happened and to find out how Penny was doing. He told me he had fed Penny cereal, but she was up asking all kinds of questions. I told him to tell her that I had an early-morning meeting and that I would be home later.

"Man, you know I never even babysat my own children, right? I am not equipped to babysit your brat all day!" Terry exclaimed. I gave Terry Ms. Blanchard's number and told him to call her and ask her to take care of Penny for the day. I sat there thinking, *How could things go so bad so fast?* Dr. Mouton interrupted my thoughts and said, "We better head over to the station."

On the way to the station, I called Coc to tell him what happened. He advised me to not say anything. He told me that he was out of the country, but he had a friend in Birmingham that could fill in for him until he arrived. I told him that I was comfortable with telling the police what happened without counsel present. He told me that I was not thinking right and that he would send his friend to meet me right away.

When we drove up to the police station, there were reporters everywhere I looked. I told Dr. Mouton that I did not want to be attacked by the mob. I called Coc and told him what happened, and he told me to go home. He said that his friend would take care of it. Coc called me back to tell me that the police agreed to meet me at my house to question me there. His friend, Royce Martin, would accompany them to my house.

When we drove up to my home, there were reporters lined up and down my street. I was confused about what to do next because Penny was in the house, and I did not want her to know what was going on. Dr. Mouton suggested that we call someone to open the garage so he could drop me off inside. I called Ms. Blanchard and once she opened the door, we quickly pulled in. Dr. Mouton told me that he had to take care of some things, but he would check on me later. I thanked him for all that he had done and closed the garage once he left.

When I walked in, Penny ran to me and grabbed my legs and said, "Hi, Brother. You're finally back. I missed you."

I picked her up, kissed her on her cheeks, and said, "I missed you, too."

"Where is My Jill?"

I looked at Ms. Blanchard, and she said, "Penny, could you help me make brownies?"

"Okay, Miss B."

I asked Ms. Blanchard to speak with her before I spoke to the police. I explained to her that the police were coming over and that I did not want Penny to see them. I would have them come through the back to interrogate me in my office. I asked her to keep Penny busy until I finished my conversation with the police.

I could not process how I felt about Jill dying, but I knew the most difficult part of my day was going to be telling Penny that Jill was never coming back. Part of me wanted to say something to protect her from knowing that Jill had died, but I knew that honesty would be best. Penny seemed to be dealing with all of the death of her loved ones better than I could ever have done.

Chapter 30

Mr. Martin, who was Coc's friend, was an older, distinguished-looking man that reminded me more of a Supreme Court Judge than a lawyer. He had a voice like the black man in the Allstate commercials. I amused myself by asking him questions that did not matter, just to hear him speak. Mr. Martin advised me not to answer any question posed by the police until he gave me a nod.

The police asked me questions like, *Why was I there so early in the morning? Did we have an argument? Did I know anyone that did not like her? Who were her closest friends, and was she having an affair?* The only questions I could answer were the ones about me being there so early in the morning and whether we'd had an argument. It did not help that her neighbors had reported hearing a man angrily yelling out Jill's name. The police became even more suspicious because I did know anything about Jill, yet we were married. They questioned our motives for getting married. I could not provide an answer to that question either.

The officers told me before they left that I should not leave town without contacting them first. I asked them again whether I was a suspect, and the female detective said, "You are the closest thing to a suspect that we have at this time."

The media grabbed hold of the story and the headline was: "Tyrese Gamble Suspect in Billionaire Wife's Death."

Tom Oreck contacted me as soon as he heard the news and told me that, the minute I found Jill, I should have contacted him. He further informed me that they take care of all players, so there would be no negative publicity connected to the team. He gave me a thirty-minute phone lecture about my responsibility to the Slammers. When he finished, I told him, in no indefinite terms, that the team was the last thing that I was concerned about under the circumstances. I'd just lost my wife and had other important family matters to deal with. He told me he was sorry for my misfortune, but that I would have a lot more worries if I did not have the financial means to take care of my family.

After all of the negative publicity was distributed around the world, it was determined that Jill died because of a brain aneurysm. However, there was not much coverage about her real cause of death. In everyone's minds, Tyrese Gamble was suspected of murdering his beautiful billionaire wife, instead of being the MVP Rookie who led his team to the first round of the playoffs. I wanted to sue the media, but Coc informed me that I did not have a case. I was in the public eye, and that came with the territory. There was nothing said that would rise to the level of libel or even slander.

I eventually told Penny about Jill's death. She took it much harder than I had expected she would. She insisted that she needed to leave me because everybody that she loved died. I immediately found a child psychologist to help her through this time. I also changed therapists because I could no longer go to Dr. Mouton's office without thinking about Jill.

I inherited all of Jill's estate. She had written a will and appointed Dr. Mouton as the executor. She included a clause in her will, that if she should marry, her spouse was to inherit her entire estate. She specifically excluded any family members, whether known or unknown. Even after the media called Jill a multi-billionaire, I did not believe it until I inherited her estate. Just to think, Coc scolded me for not getting a prenup, when, in reality, she was the one most at risk and who should have protected her assets.

Something in me wanted to find Jill's mother to let her know that her daughter had died. However, with all of the news surrounding her death, I would have been surprised if she did not already know. When I asked Coc to find out, I was shocked to hear that Jill's mom had died a year ago from breast cancer. I wanted to somehow honor Jill, so I used some of the inheritance to assist Italian immigrants who needed financial assistance to get started in America. Jill was proud of her Italian heritage, and I thought this would have been something she would have endorsed.

****

The summer was very busy for us. Penny and I spent the summer redecorating her room and my room; we made her a playroom and created a room for her nanny. I found a great nanny, Patrice, who had recently graduated with a B.S. in child development. Patrice was uncertain about what she wanted to do with her major, but she knew that she loved children. She told me that she definitely would be commit to me for at least two years, because she was going to enroll in an online graduate degree program. I was happy because she was great with Penny, and Penny adored her.

My therapy for dealing with Jill's death was to bury myself in work. Bart and I worked together on my non-profit and successfully solicited professional athletes to endorse the program and work with some of our kids. With the exception of the owners of the team, I experienced much love and support from my basketball family. The wives of some of the players came over to help me with Penny when they found out what happened. They arranged play dates where they would pick up Penny and take her on adventures with their children.

By the end of summer, Penny and I had a large support group that made certain that her every need was attended to. I was confident that, by the time I started practicing for the pre-season, Penny would be completely settled into her new life.

Coc paid Tyrone so that he would never contact us again. Son, like father. I knew he did not want Penny;

he was only interested in money. Penny rarely asked for anyone other than Mammy, and I made certain that she spoke with Mammy often. I promised Penny, prior to starting school, we would go and visit Mammy. Two weeks before school was to start, Penny and I prepared for our trip to Port Arthur. I called Aunt Verdie to let her know that we were coming to Houston to spend some time with her.

We were waiting for our baggage at the airport when a lady caught my eye. She was walking toward the baggage claim area. She walked with such confidence that I just stopped what I was doing and stared. As she came closer, I recognized her. It was Porchia. I had not spoken to Porchia since Vegas.

She walked right past us. I shouted, "Pocahontas!"

She jumped and said, "Hi, Ty. I am sorry I did not see you. My mind was elsewhere. How are you?"

We embraced and I said, "I am fine. You look great."

"You look great, also. Hey! I have been meaning to call you to give you my condolences for the loss of your wife."

"No, I understand. I have been crazy busy myself."

Penny interrupted our reunion by saying, "It is so cool that your name is Pocahontas. You look just like her!"

Porchia smiled and said, "Well, hello there. My name is really Porchia. What is your name?"

Penny said, "My name is Penny. But I prefer Pocahontas over Porchia."

Porchia looked at Penny and said, "Well, Penny, it is a pleasure to meet you. And if you prefer Pocahontas, you can call me Pocahontas."

"Pocahontas, this is my little sister. I have to apologize for her directness. She's quite assertive and has never meets a stranger," I said, laughing.

Porchia laughed, then she said, "Well, it must run in the family."

Penny then said, "So are you going to Aunt Verdie's with us?"

"Well, I don't live far from your aunt Verdie."

"Well, can you come and visit us?"

"I will see what I can do Penny."

I knew that if I did not stop Penny, she would go on with other questions, so I quickly said, "Well, Porchia, it looked as if you were on a mission. It was nice seeing you, and hopefully I will see you again soon."

Penny blurted, "I would like to see you again soon too Pocahontas!"

Porchia looked at Penny and said, "Okay. I will make that happen Ms. Penny."

I stood and shrugged my shoulders, and Porchia just smiled and said, "See you Ty."

Chapter 31

Penny and Aunt Verdie were running things at the house. I definitely felt like an outsider. We were all sitting around the table, and Aunt Verdie and Penny were playing a card game that Aunt Verdie had probably made up, as she had done when we were kids. There was a knock on the door. I looked and asked, "Is Poo Man back?"

Aunt Verdie said, "When has that boy has ever knocked on the door? Even when he forgets his key. He hollers, 'Mama! Mama!' for me to get up and open the door."

Aunt Verdie was about to get up, but I told her that I would get it.

When I walked to the door, I was surprised to see Porchia standing there with a wrapped gift. I opened the door and said, "Hi, there. What a pleasant surprise! It is not my birthday!"

Porchia hugged me and said, "This is not for you. This is a gift for Penny."

"Her birthday is not until next month," I said.

"Stop tripping. This is just a 'nice to meet you' gift," said Porchia.

"Don't spoil her. I have to raise her."

"Does she live with you?" Porchia asked, surprisingly.

"Yes, she does."

"Wow! I am impressed. How is that working out?"

"We are working it out together."

"Well, I am proud of you! Raising a child is one of the most important jobs a person can have. It takes love, time, support, and dedication. And with your schedule, I know it can't be easy."

"Penny makes it easy. She is a great child."

"Yeah, in the brief moment I met her, she captured my heart."

"She has a way of doing that to everyone."

"So I guess you don't have much time for dating these days."

"I don't have much time for anything. But Penny has the best nanny. She has been a lifesaver."

"Well, where is the cutie now?"

"Come on. She is in the kitchen with Aunt Verdie."

When we walked into the kitchen, Penny ran to Porchia and said, "Oh, Pocahontas, you came!"

"Of course. I told you that I would. And here is something for you."

"Oh, thank you Pocahontas!"

Penny tore into the gift, and it was a children's Bible.

Penny ran and hugged Porchia and said, "Oh, I have always wanted my own bible. Thanks!"

Penny enjoyed going to Sunday school and church, so I knew that she was excited about getting a Bible.

She would ask both me and Patrice to read her bible stories.

"Well, if you are around Penny, I could take you to church with me on Sunday?"

"I would love that. Can Brother go also?"

"Of course, Brother is welcome to come."

Porchia went and hugged Aunt Verdie and told her it was nice to see her again. Aunt Verdie asked Porchia whether she wanted something to eat, and Porchia said she had just eaten. They talked about Poo Man while Penny excitedly looked through her Bible. I just sat back and watched it all. Everyone looked happy in that moment. I felt happy, just observing. I wished that I could have frozen that moment.

Porchia called me Saturday night to find out if it was okay to take Penny to Sunday school and church the next day. I told her, only if she agreed to have dinner with me before I left. She said she was not one for blackmail, but since she could not afford a nice dinner, she would gladly take me up on my offer. I was happy that she agreed, because I knew no one could make Porchia Williams do anything that she did not want to do; regardless of her circumstances.

Penny came back very excited about attending church with Porchia and somebody named, Pastor Sadiq. I tried not to interrogate my eight-year-old sister, but I had to find out more about this Pastor Sadiq. According to Penny, Pastor Sadiq had driven them to church. Afterward, they went to eat at some place that had a lot of rides and games. I became angry when I found out that Porchia had Penny around some other man. But I did not want to upset Penny, so I stopped asking questions.

Porchia and I had previously made a date for Monday night, and I could not wait to get her in front of me to find out the deal with her and Pastor Sadiq. I knew that it was unreasonable for me to be upset about anything that Porchia did, but I could not help it. Yeah, I know I had gotten married, but it was only her that I ever wanted. She was the one who had written me off. I never stopped wanting or loving her. When I pulled up to the house, Porchia was standing there talking to a lady. She kissed the lady and started walking toward the car. I jumped out and greeted her with a kiss on the cheek and opened her door.

"Was that Mystery?" I asked.

"No, that is my Aunt Char. She lives in my house."

"I didn't know that you had an aunt."

"Neither did I. It's a long story. I'm thinking about writing a book about it," she said and laughed.

"And her name is Char?"

"No, it's really Chardonnay. I call her Char for short."

I laughed and said, "Only you would have an aunt named after a wine."

"Watch yourself. You will get cut up talking about my family," Porchia said, smiling.

"Oh, I see you still have that violent streak. Has that seminary taught you anything?"

"Yep! How to cut you up without using a knife," she laughed.

"You were already an expert at doing that," I responded.

By the time we arrived to the restaurant, Porchia had filled me in on what she had been doing over the last year. However, she never once mentioned Pastor Sadiq. I would have to find out a way to bring him up during dinner.

The waiter came and asked us if we wanted something to drink. I looked at Porchia and she said, "Yes, what red wines would you suggest?"

The waiter rambled off several of their red wines, and she picked a bottle of cabernet sauvignon from France that had been aged for ten years. I wondered whether she was serious about not being able to afford dinner. I looked at her and said, "I think I like it better when you are taking shots of tequila."

"Oh, are you trying to take advantage of me tonight?"

"Would you let me?"

"Ty! You know I am a Christian woman."

"So does that mean that you don't enjoy your life?"

"No, that means that I follow His word. And I do not believe that the Bible condones fornication."

I sighed and said, "Good! That means that you are not giving up my stuff to Pastor Sadiq."

Porchia stared at me for a while before speaking. She said, "I don't think you have the right to tell me who I can or cannot sleep with. I guess you don't remember calling me to tell me that you were married."

"Well, you made it clear to me that you were not interested in me."

"Okay, so what's changed besides your wife dying?"

I saw that our food was coming to the table, so I said, "Woo! Saved by the food!"

Porchia looked at me with a troubled look on her face and said, "Sorry Ty for that comment. It was out-of-line and that was very insensitive of me."

I changed the conversation to lighter topics. We got through dinner without addressing what I really wanted to discuss.

The waiter came over and asked whether we would like dessert. I responded, "Yes, but the beautiful lady probably won't let me get it."

I looked at Porchia with a smirk and asked, "Would you like dessert, dear?"

She looked and said, "Dessert is not good for me. I will pass."

I looked at the waiter and said, "I think we will both pass this time. Can I have the bill, sir?"

Porchia looked at me and said, "Okay, there is an elephant in the room."

"Well, he is not in the room right now. But evidently he went to church with you and Penny."

"Ty, not that it is any of your business. But Sadiq is just a friend. He has been supportive of me through my transition."

"I would like to be supportive of you through your transition."

"No Ty. You want more. I don't think you know how to be a friend."

The waiter came over with the bill, and Porchia grabbed it and asked the waiter to wait as she gave him her credit card.

"What was that all about?" I asked.

"Just felt like treating you this time."

"I think that was a move to get me off the subject. But whether you know it or not, I can be a great friend."

"Yeah, you probably could be a great friend. But I am talking about you being a great friend to me. We have not spoken since Vegas, and you are acting as if I have been cheating on you."

"You are right. I do feel as if you are cheating on me. You are cheating me out of the opportunity to make you happy. You are cheating us out of the life we deserve together."

"Ty, this is just not the time. I am doing what I need to do for myself right now. Can you respect that?"

"I have been respecting that, but I want more. Can we at least talk from time-to-time?"

"Yes, we can talk. But I am not ready for a relationship."

"Okay, that is enough for me right now."

Chapter 32

We went to visit Mammy. I was going to stay at the Hampton Inn in Port Arthur, but Penny begged me to stay with her. She had lost so many people and did not like me to be out of her sight for too long, so I agreed to stay with her at Mammy's. We were supposed to stay for only two days, but I knew that it would be difficult for me to stay even one more night.

I was so tired of ducking the flying roaches. I had to sleep completely clothed, afraid of what types of insects and rodents might attack me while I slept. I did not like the conditions that Mammy was living in. I did not think an elder should have to live like this. We had a discussion about who took of her, and she told me she basically took care of herself. I asked Mammy, "If I find you a nice place to live, would you move there?"

She told me that she did not want to go and rot away at an old folks' home.

I decided to extend our stay to find Mammy a suitable place to live. I could not find any acceptable independent living facilities in Port Arthur, but I found a beautiful home that Mammy loved in Beaumont. It was still close enough for anyone that wanted to see her from Port Arthur could do so. The apartments were located on a lake and included all types of activities for seniors.

While visiting the retirement community, Mammy smiled the entire time. It just so happened that they had a two-bedroom apartment that was vacant. Mammy decided that she would move, so I made arrangements to pay for her to live in the community. I assured her that we would visit her as much as possible. I told her that I still owned a home in Beaumont and visited Houston quite often.

Once we got Mammy all settled, Penny and I headed back to Birmingham. Before I could get on the plane, I received a call from Tyrelle Jr. He thanked me for moving his grandmother. He told me that he should be getting out of jail in another six months, and he would help take care of her. He realized that I did not have any obligation to take care of her, and he could not thank me enough. I told him that anybody that Penny cared about, I also cared about. I told him that, when he got out of jail, I would be willing to help him, if he was willing to help himself.

I realized, after I hung up, that I did not know anything about him. I hoped I was not getting myself into something that I would regret. I called Coc to get as much information on Tyrelle Jr. as possible. After hanging up with Coc, I realized that my family issues alone could support Coc and his lifestyle.

Penny fell asleep once Terry picked us up from the airport. Terry brought in the luggage while I took Penny upstairs to her room. When I came back downstairs, Terry was standing with a very serious look on his face. He said, "Hey, T. Man, I need to talk to you."

"Can it wait 'til tomorrow?"

He looked at me hesitantly and said, "I guess."

I saw the anxious look on his face, so I said, "If it is that important, we can talk now. I just want to make sure I get Penny situated."

"Nah man. It can wait. I'll see you tomorrow."

"All right. Be careful out there."

"Fa sho bro," Terry said as he walked out the door.

When I went back upstairs to check on Penny, I ran into Patrice coming out of Penny's room.

"Is she still sleeping?" I asked.

"Yeah, she is out. I did not want to wake her to make her take a bath. Did you all have a good trip?"

"It was a long one. I am glad to be back home."

"Well, I need to speak with you about something."

"Don't tell me that you are leaving us. I could not handle that."

"Well, not yet. But how would you feel if I still did everything I did, but no longer lived here?"

"What?"

"Yes, I could be available from six in the morning until Penny goes to bed."

"What? You don't like the premises?"

"I love it. But I've met someone."

"So what ... you are moving in with this someone?"

"Yes, I would like to see how it works out," she said.

"Patrice, let's go to my office to discuss this."

She followed me, and once we got in the office she said, "He said you would not like it."

"Who is he?"

"Terry."

"What? You are seeing Terry?"

"Yes, we're a couple."

"Wait! Why do you want to move in with him? Why can't you date him without moving in with him?"

"We want to see if we are compatible."

"Patrice, I think you are rushing into something that you don't know anything about?"

"Sir, not to disrespect you, but you are not my daddy. I am a grown woman. I can make my own decisions."

"Okay, why don't I speak with both you and Terry together?"

I picked up the office phone and dialed Terry's number. His voice mail answered, and I hollered, "Get yo' ass back over here right now!" Then I hung up the phone.

Patrice looked at me and said, "Mr. Gamble, why would you speak like that to him? This is something that we both want. It is something positive. I won't neglect any of my responsibilities to Penny. I promise!"

I tried to calm myself down. I said to her, "Let's discuss this when Terry arrives."

Patrice stormed out of my office like a ten-year-old.

I knew things about Terry that she did not know. He ran through women like I ran through sneakers. I could not believe he was messing around with my nanny. He knew the rule about not pissing in the pot that fed you. She was a great nanny, and I could not afford to lose her or have his sorry ass mess things up.

Terry showed up two hours later. Ms. Blanchard let him in, and I walked out and shouted, "Back here!"

He walked into my office and said, "What's up?"

"Nicca, don't act like you don't know what's up!"

"Why are you tripping? You fucking her too!"

"You can act simple if you want to, but you know it ain't about that dog. You know you are not supposed to fuck with the help!"

"And it ain't like that with her. I really am interested in her."

"Interested! What the fuck does that mean?"

Patrice came in with an angry look on her face and shouted, "Mr. Gamble, if you don't approve of us, I will quit and move in with him anyway!"

I looked at Terry, then Terry looked back at Patrice, and said, "Baby, let me handle this. And please close the door on your way out."

Terry looked at me and whispered, "I think I am catching feelings for her."

I looked at him and said, "Okay. Here's the deal. You can do what you want. But if she ends up fucking over Penny. You're outta here!"

"Dog how you gonna do that to me? I have been here for you."

"I should be asking you that," I said.

"Okay. Okay. I'll figure out something."

A few days later, Terry set it up where Patrice caught him with another chic. She broke it off with him and apologized to me for making a rash decision.

I had a conversation with her and told her that she should move slower with love next time. I told her she needed to get to know the guy before deciding to make a big decision like moving in with him. All I knew was that Penny needed her right now, and I would do anything to keep her. I could not allow Penny to keep losing people she loved. I needed to protect her at any cost, even if it meant denying her nanny from potential love. But I really did not think that Terry had her best interest at heart. He probably would have gotten bored with her and tossed her out like he had done with the many that had come before her.

Patrice got over losing Terry and started putting all of her time and effort back into Penny. She started the journey of the much-needed school shopping and getting Penny prepared for going to school with wealthy kids. As part of school shopping, I asked Patrice to also buy Penny a top of the line desktop computer and a good Android phablet, so she could stay in touch with me at all times. Going to private school was going to be a big shift from the public schools that Penny had attended in Port Arthur. However, Penny was bright, so I knew she could compete with those kids on any level. She was very articulate, assertive, and intelligent. I just wanted to make sure her integration into her new environment was without any problems.

Chapter 33

Just as I was settling into my role as a big brother-daddy, I had to get back into being Tyrese Gamble, the basketball player. We had lost two of our starters, so it was difficult to get back into the role of playing together as a team. I was struggling personally because I did not do as much training in my off season as I typically would have done.

I had to put more effort into getting into shape. And to make matters even worse, I was horny. I don't ever recall a time in my life that I was horny most of the time. I found myself having sex with groupies at any opportunity I could get. It was difficult because I was in and out of hotels. I could not bring these women around Penny and did not like the idea of being away from Penny when I was not taking care of business or on the court.

Porchia and I had only talked a couple of times, and she would repeat her mantra to me: "I am doing me." I knew I wanted more, so I gave her the space that she needed. Having sex with various women did not fulfill me, and I felt bad because I knew they wanted more. I treated each of them with respect. I would wine and dine them, but I usually did not go out any of them more than once. When I did go out on more than one date, they always misread my intentions. There was too much drama associated with trying to keep one woman on booty call mode.

I became bored with the women, so I started spending time in the underground of Atlanta. I had several boys that would service me regularly. I was more into oral sex being performed on me than anything else. I would only engage in sex when it was someone I knew had as much to lose as I did. I even spent time with Jeremy, the chef in Vegas, from time-to-time. I would fly him to Atlanta for a weekend of sex. When he started wanting more, I told him I could not give him more. He threatened to reveal what I was doing, so I kicked him to the curb. I knew I could never have another crazy Raheem in my life. Luckily, Jeremy never followed through with his threats.

I often thought about what my life would have been like married to Jill. I probably would have been living as a happy heterosexual husband and dad. These days, I found myself switching between torrid affairs with women and men. I did not like myself, and I definitely wanted to be different for Penny's sake. I wanted to provide her with an example of what a loving relationship was like, so that, as an adult, she would have a positive role model to emulate. But at this time, the only thing I could do was love her and show her that a man should always treat her as the princess she is.

Penny seemed to be adjusting well to her new school. She spent many weekends doing social things with her friends from school. She had two besties, as they called themselves, Beck (Rebecca) and Kel (Kelly). And, of course, she was Pen to them. I was hesitant to let her stay anywhere overnight, so many times, their sleepovers were at our house, and Patrice would plan a weekend full of activities that would keep them busy.

When we played in town, they would have floor seats at the Slammers games. For Penny's birthday, we surprised her by letting her think that for her birthday, they were going to the movies. When she returned to the house, there were about thirty kids waiting for a swim party. At the end of the night, she declared, "Brother, this is the best party ever!"

Penny had an open house at her school where, for the first time, I was not out of town at a game, so instead of Patrice attending, I attended. Penny was very excited about me meeting Ms. Pollock. I was shocked when I arrived and met Ms. Pollock. I had pictured Ms. Pollock as a young blonde who was a size 0 with a flat azz.

Instead, Ms. Pollock resembled Angie Stone. She was tall, voluptuous, and gorgeous. I had never dated anyone who was more than a size eight, but she worked a size eighteen well. She wore her hair natural, which added to her appeal. She looked at me and said, as Penny would have said, "It is finally nice to meet you, Brother."

I laughed and said, "The pleasure is all mine Teacher."

We sat, and she told me how impressed she was with Penny. She actually thought that, academically, she was on a fifth grade level, instead of a fourth grade level. However, she thought that she was better off with kids her age because she was not as mature as a lot of her peers and that she too easily trusted others. She went on to tell me that some kids would try to get Penny to do things that were not in her best interest.

I asked her to be more specific. She said that one of the boys once told Penny that he had the same private part that she did. And she tried to convince him that they had different private parts. So he asked her to prove it to him. So she pulled down her pants and panties, so he could see that their private parts were different.

When she told me that story, it took me back to my Rico days. She said that several incidents such as that had happened because Penny thought that everyone was doing things in good faith. I thanked her for having this frank discussion with me and urged her to call me right away when she had any information like this or knew of anything that might affect Penny's well-being. I gave her my number, and she gave me her number to contact her if I had any concerns as well. When we got in the car, Penny looked at me and said, "Brother, I am glad that you met Ms. Pollock."

"Yes, I am glad that I met her too," I said.

Then I asked, "Princess, do people make you do things that end up getting you in trouble?"

"Um. Yes. Sometimes."

"If something does not sound right, you should not do it."

"But it does not usually sound like it's wrong."

"Princess, if someone wants to see your private part or touches you on your private parts, that's wrong. And you need to tell me!"

I realized I had screamed at her, so I tried to get my emotions under control.

She looked up at me with tears forming in her eyes and said, "Okay, Brother. I am sorry."

"You don't have to apologize. I just want you to understand and to let me know if something like that ever happens. Has anyone ever touched you on your private parts?"

"Yes."

My heart stopped, and I hesitantly asked, "Who, sweetie?"

"My mom when she would bathe me when I was little."

"Besides that?"

"No, Brother."

I let out a big sigh of relief and said, "Okay, don't show anyone your private parts for any reason. Do you understand?"

"Yes, Brother."

On the drive home, my head exploded with thoughts of what Rico did to me. I could not ever let anything like that happen to Penny. I did not understand how she could be so naïve. Then I thought about me not knowing what to do to a girl when I was in junior high school. I was going to need to have a discussion with her about sex, but I was not ready for that. I decided to discuss with Penny's therapist the best way to have this discussion.

When I saw Patrice, I remembered that she had majored in child development, so she would definitely be able to help. She said she had some books that had been specifically written for pre-teens about sex. She said that she could share those books with Penny. I told her that I wanted to see them before she gave them to Penny. She told me that she was more than qualified to have the discussion, but she would practice on me first.

When she read the book to me, I thought it was a little too much information for a nine year old, but I was not qualified in the area. Patrice explained to me that she would also be equipped to answer any questions that Penny may have about what she was discussing. I was glad that the book addressed inappropriate sexual behavior, and I was glad that it had some helpful tips on Internet safety.

I had censored and blocked certain channels on the TV, but I had not blocked certain programs on Penny's computer or phone. I asked Patrice to make certain that Penny could only access only kid-friendly programs and that we had the proper protections on all of her social media accounts.

I also took her phone and programmed it for her to be able to only call certain people and to allow only certain people to call her. Her phone list was limited to Mammy, Aunt Verdie, Patrice, Terry, Porchia, Rebecca, Kelly, and me. If she wanted another name added, I explained to her that she would have to come to me to get permission. It may have been overkill, but I wanted to, not only inform Penny about the ills of society, but protect her as much as possible from predators.

Chapter 34

Ms. Pollock called me to let me know that Penny was being a lot wiser when dealing with her peers.

I said, "Well, I am glad to hear that, Ms. Pollock. Is she still doing okay academically?

"Yes, she is. But please call me Deidra."

"Then, Deidra, I have a question for you?"

"Yes?"

"Where did you get the last name Pollock?"

"From my adopted father. My mother married Jim Pollock, and he adopted me."

"Oh, so your mom married a white man?"

"Yes, his family is from Scotland."

"Wow! I totally pictured you wrong."

"Most people do."

"So, Ms. Pollock."

She stopped me in the middle of my sentence and said, "Deidra."

"I'm sorry, Deidra. Are you allowed to date your students' parents?"

"Probably not. But I don't think there is anything against dating my student's brother."

"Ah, you are a smart one. Well if that's the case, I'd like to take you out."

"Hmmm ... let me think about that. Sure," she said.

"Are you available tomorrow?" I asked.

"After five," she responded.

"Okay, can you text me your address? I will pick you up at six."

"Okay, I'll see you then, Mr. Gamble."

"Oh, I have to call you Deidra, while you get to call me Mr. Gamble?"

"I can always call you Brother, if you'd like."

"Okay, I'm about tired of you making fun of my sister. But you can call me Ty for now. But I'm certain after our first date, you'll be calling me Daddy."

She laughed and said, "All right, player. I will see you tomorrow."

"Looking forward to it."

I thought about our date and wanted to do something different. I was tired of movies and dinner, drinks and a club; I wanted to be original. I hoped that she enjoyed a little physical activity.

When I went to her house, she had on a form-fitting jumpsuit and heels. She looked absolutely delicious. The jumpsuit outlined every one of her great curves. I know my eyes told her that I appreciated her outfit, but my lips had to tell her that where we were going, it was more appropriate if she wore jeans, a T-shirt, and tennis shoes. She gave me a strange look, then invited me into her house while she changed. She came back in leggings, a T-shirt, and Timberlands. She still looked hot.

I drove us to the Paintball Play House, and she looked at me and said, "This is gonna be cool. And I am gonna kick your ass."

I looked at her and said, "What happened to the prim and proper Ms. Pollock?"

She shook her head and said, "Tonight, you are dealing with yo' homegirl DeDe. Now come on, so I can shoot yo' ass."

I could not believe how competitive Deidra was. She definitely was serious about winning. But it was the most fun I'd had on a date in a while. After she'd kicked my butt in three games, I felt like I could not go home without being victorious.

I asked, "How about we go bowling?"

"Oh, Tyrese Gamble knows how to bowl? I thought that was the working man's game."

"Don't let the bling fool you," I said, laughing.

I called one of my teammates who had a mini regulation-sized bowling alley at his house, and he told me it was cool to come over.

I introduced Deidra to his wife. After they exchanged pleasantries, I told them I needed to use the lane to show Deidra who was the man. Deidra smiled and said, "Yeah, I just kicked his butt at paintball, so he feels that he needs to beat me at something."

My teammate led us to the bowling alley and put everything into action, so we could bowl. He looked at Deidra and said, "Kick his butt again!"

She responded, "No doubt."

I won the first game, but she won the next two. I told her that our next date would be on the basketball court. She told me that I would lose there, too.

We rolled up to Deidra's house, and I got out to open the door for her. Before I could get around to her door, she opened it and said, "That is very chivalrous of you, but I can open my own door."

I backed up and said, "Well, excuse me Ms. Independent."

I walked her to her door and hoped that she would invite me in, but she looked at me and said, "Well, this is the end of the line."

"Oh, you are not inviting me in?"

"No sir. But I had a wonderful evening. This is, by far, the best date I have had in a while. I really enjoyed myself."

"I enjoyed myself also," I said as I leaned in to kiss her.

She raised her hand up for me to kiss her hand.

I said, "Hey! I thought you were not into chivalry."

"I'm not, but I am not into kissing on a first date either."

"Wow! No kissing?"

"No sir. No kissing," she said.

"Wow! How many dates until a kiss?" I asked.

Then, all of a sudden she grabbed me and gave me a long, sensual kiss.

She said, "Now you can get over not being kissed, and we can move on to just enjoying each other's company."

"Well, if that is the case, why can't we just get over the sex part too?"

She started unlocking her door and then, once she opened it, she looked at me and said, "I see, when you get an inch, you try to take miles. But you are going to have to slow yo' roll partna. You 'bout three dates ahead with that kiss."

"Ha! It would have taken three dates for a kiss?"

"Yes, at a minimum."

"Wow! Okay. I'll take that. I really enjoyed myself. Can't wait to do it again," I said.

"Me too. But you might want to practice first if it is going to involve any type of competitive sport."

"Ha! I will remember that. Goodnight Miss Competitive."

"Goodnight, Mr. Loser."

I walked away, and she did not close her door until I got into my car. I really enjoyed my date with Deidra. Before I could start my car, I received a text that read, "Thanks for the night. And please let me know when you make it back home. DeDe."

I had never had a woman ask me to let her know when I got home. But I was glad to know that she cared. As I was driving home, I thought about Penny. I knew that she adored Ms. Pollock, but I wondered how she would feel about me dating her.

Chapter 35

I had been dating Deidra exclusively for four months, but we still had not had sex. We both decided to keep our relationship away from Penny. I knew that, if Penny knew, she would reveal our relationship to everyone. She was sweet, but could not hold back any information. Plus, I did not want to bring another woman into Penny's life without knowing whether she was going to be around for a long time.

Deidra did not want to give the administration any reason to doubt her objectivity when it came to teaching her students. She also convinced me that it was best for Penny to remain in her class. She was not certain about the qualifications of the other fourth grade teachers to properly deal with Penny as the only African-American female at the school.

I let everyone go, even my boy toys, for an opportunity to have something real with Deidra. I would not go so far and marry her like I did Jill, but I think that she could be a positive influence for both me and Penny. Everything I did was for the benefit of Penny.

One day, Penny shocked me. She told me that she had been talking to Pocahontas about God and Jesus, and she wanted to be baptized. I did not have any idea that she had been in communication with Porchia.

"So how often do you speak with Pocahontas?"

"She calls me on Fridays to see how my week has gone?"

"Really? Does she ask about me?"

"Yeah, she sometimes asks how you are doing."

"Why didn't you tell me that you talk with Pocahontas?"

"I did not think I had to. Everyone in my phone, you gave me permission to speak with," responded Penny.

She caught me off guard with her answer. But I followed up with, "What do you talk about?"

"No specific subject. Things like school, my friends, church, Patrice, Mammy, Jesus, and stuff like that," she said.

"Well, I am glad that you talk with her."

"Brother, why don't you marry Pocahontas, so she can be with us?"

I wanted to say, *Why don't you ask Pocahontas?* But instead I said, "Because Pocahontas is trying to accomplish something very important. And she needs to be where she is to accomplish it."

"So maybe when she is done, you can marry her."

"We will see. Have you done all of your homework?"

"Yes."

"Okay Princess. I think it is bedtime for you."

"Will you read me a story tonight?"

"Sure," I said.

She handed me the Bible that Porchia had given her and told me to read the part about Jesus getting baptized by John. I was not sure where that story was, but I eventually found it in the third chapter of Matthew.

After Penny fell asleep in my arms, I gently placed her on her pillow, covered her up, and then turned off her lights. She insisted that her door stay open. I wondered how long she would sleep with her door open. I knew most kids did not want their parents in their room, so not only did they close the door, they had locks. I could only hope that she stayed sweet, young, and innocent.

After retiring to my bedroom, I could not help but think about Porchia. Maybe there was hope since she stayed in contact with Penny. I did not want to get my hopes too high because I knew Penny had a way of making folks fall in love with her. Porchia had made it clear to me many times that she was not interested in anything serious. I knew that my only choice, at this time, was to live my life and hope that perhaps one day our lives would join. My thoughts about Porchia were interrupted with a call from Deidra.

I answered, and Deidra said, "Hey, Chocolate Thunder. I think it is time for our bodies to be joined."

TO BE CONTINUED...

If Loving Me is Wrong

Porchia is coming back to close out the Porchia Tetralogy. Yes, some have said that I leave my readers hanging. You will no longer be hanging with the final book narrated by Porchia, *If Loving Me is Wrong*. Porchia will take you through her college years up until. Oh no, you know I am not going to tell you what happens. But I will tell you that it'll keep you on the edge of your seat. All of your favorite characters are returning: Mystery, Ty, Pastor Sadiq, Tracy, Sweezy, Chardonnay, Penny, and a few new and intriguing characters.

If this is your first time being exposed to a JJV: The Storyteller novel, you must also read:

Can't Nobody (Book 1)
&
The Dubois Curse (Book 2)

243